"...er what
...d never
...to be
..., Akira.
...I know that
...ght feels the same.
Don't you?"

- Amelia Rosequartz

→ Asahina Kyousuke

"It seems I might just be able to take down both of these things by myself after all!"

Amaryllis looked down at the ring again—only this time, her gaze was charged with mana.

"What a fascinating magical device you have there. Correct me if I'm wrong, but couldn't you just use that to solve our current predicament?"

→Amaryllis Cluste

My Status *as an* Assassin *Obviously* Exceeds *the* Hero's

NOVEL

4

WRITTEN BY
Matsuri Akai

ILLUSTRATED BY
Tozai

Airship

Seven Seas Entertainment

CONTENTS

ANSATSUSHA DE ARU ORE NO SUTETASU GA YUUSHA
YORI MO AKIRAKA NI TSUYOI NODAGA VOL. 4
© 2021 Matsuri Akai
Illustrated by Tozai
First published in Japan in 2021 by OVERLAP Inc., Ltd., Tokyo.
English translation rights arranged with OVERLAP Inc., Ltd., Tokyo.

Seven Seas press and purchase enquiries can be sent to
Marketing Manager Lianne Sentar at press@gomanga.com.
Information regarding the distribution and purchase of
digital editions is available from Digital Manager CK Russell
at digital@gomanga.com.

Follow Seven Seas Entertainment online at
sevenseasentertainment.com.

TRANSLATION: Colby W.
ADAPTATION: Leigh Teetzel
COVER DESIGN: H. Qi
INTERIOR DESIGN: Clay Gardner
INTERIOR LAYOUT: Brennan Thome
COPY EDITOR: Jade Gardner
PROOFREADER: T. Anne
LIGHT NOVEL EDITOR: Mercedez Clewis
PREPRESS TECHNICIAN: Melanie Ujimori
PRINT MANAGER: Rhiannon Rasmussen-Silverstein
PRODUCTION MANAGER: Lissa Pattillo
EDITOR-IN-CHIEF: Julie Davis
ASSOCIATE PUBLISHER: Adam Arnold
PUBLISHER: Jason DeAngelis

ISBN: 978-1-63858-195-6
Printed in Canada
First Printing: April 2022
10 9 8 7 6 5 4 3 2 1

CHARACTERS

CROW

Retired member of the previous hero's party. Class: Blacksmith. Has agreed to serve as the party's guide through the demons' domain in exchange for Akira assassinating the man who killed his sister.

NIGHT

A familiar with whom Akira has forged a pact. Was once the Demon Lord's right-hand monster. Can transform into other monsters at will via his Shapeshifter ability.

ODA AKIRA

An ordinary high schooler who was summoned to the world of Morrigan. Class: Assassin. On a quest to avenge Knight Commander Saran and find a way home to Japan.

SATOU TSUKASA

One of Akira's classmates. Class: Hero. Has had a complicated relationship with Akira ever since childhood but is now traveling with him toward the Demon Lord's castle in search of a way back home.

LIA LAGOON

Princess of the beastfolk nation of Uruk. Class: Guardian. Is currently investigating the hero summoning ritual because she suspects it had something to do with the destruction of her village.

AMELIA ROSEQUARTZ

Princess of the elves. Class: Spirit Medium. Was rescued by Akira from the belly of a black slime deep in the labyrinth. Has traveled with him ever since.

ASAHINA KYOUSUKE

A member of the hero's party. Class: Samurai. One of Akira's only true friends. Wields Hakuryuu, the companion blade to Akira's Yato-no-Kami.

LATTICENAIL

Daughter of the Demon Lord. Class: Water/ Fire Mage. Doesn't get along well with the Demon Lord, so she ran away from home, at which point she met Akira and company.

NANASE RINTAROU

A member of the hero's party. Class: Wind Mage. With his superb communication skills, he serves as a mediator of sorts for the party.

TSUDA TOMOYA

A member of the hero's party. Class: Knight. Has a bit of a complex about his more feminine aspects. Aspires to one day be as strong as Kyousuke.

WAKI DAISUKE

A member of the hero's party. Class: Animal Trainer. An easygoing (if simpleminded) boy who can always lighten the party's mood.

HOSOYAMA SHIORI

A member of the hero's party. Class: Healer. An attractive girl with a soft demeanor but a strong will. Has known Yuki since childhood.

UENO YUKI

A member of the hero's party. Class: Disenchanter. A girl who speaks with a Kansai accent and is all pep, all the time. Has known Shiori since childhood.

GILLES ASTI

The former Vice Commander of the Knights of Retice. Class: Knight. Hoping to carry out the late Commander Saran's will, he now travels with the party as a concerned chaperone of sorts.

EDMOND ROSE RETICE

King of the human nation of Retice. Claims to be using the hero summoning ritual in order to thwart the Demon Lord, but it seems his true motivations lie elsewhere...

MARIA ROSE RETICE

Princess of the human nation of Retice. On her father's orders, she placed a brainwashing curse on Akira's classmates.

Illustrations by **Tozai**

My Status as an
Assassin Obviously
Exceeds *the* Hero's

The Story So Far

SOME TIME AGO, an ordinary high schooler by the name of Oda Akira found himself summoned (along with his classmates) against his will into the Kingdom of Retice, a nation in a world completely separate from his own. Here, he was granted the class of Assassin—yet he was even stronger than his classmate who had been dubbed the Hero. Not one who liked standing out, Akira quickly hid himself in the background, and with a lot of help from Knight Commander Saran, Akira began to develop the strength he'd need to get by in this dangerous world. However, not long after discovering that he and his classmates were being used in a diabolical plot by the king of Retice, Akira was framed for Commander Saran's murder. Having no choice but to flee the country, Akira hid within a great labyrinth nearby. It was in the depths of this labyrinth that he saved an elven princess named Amelia from the belly of a pitch-black slime, and she became his loyal companion. Then, after defeating the feline boss monster, Night, on the lowest floor, Akira made a pact with the beast and Night became his familiar.

After Night revealed that the Demon Lord awaits him in his castle, Akira set forth on a journey with his new companions—first to the elven domain, then to the land of the beastfolk. On the elven continent, he helped Amelia reconcile with her younger sister, Kilika, and in the port town of Ur on the beastfolk continent, he and his companions helped stave off a surprise attack by demons. Not long after that, in the town of Mali in the beastfolk nation of Uruk, Akira was tasked with the assassination of the Uruk guildmaster—a man named Gram, who was using the annual beauty pageant as a front to commit horrific crimes. Initially quite conflicted about this job, Akira eventually found the resolve he needed to carry out the hit after learning Gram was the true puppet master behind Commander Saran's death.

Our story picks up just after said assassination has been successfully carried out—but Akira still has mixed feelings, for this was the first time he's ever had to kill another sentient being...

A Glimpse of the Future

"THIS IS THE END for you! Roaring Thunder!!!"

The demon raised his arms to the heavens and then brought them crashing back down. Rays of brilliant, dazzling light burst forth from a giant magic circle lined with complex runes, and the man could feel the impact of the attack coursing through his outstretched arm as he braced against the onslaught. A blinding, white light flashed through the entire area before eventually abating. The man coughed in the resulting cloud of dust and then let out a sigh, almost sounding disappointed.

When the dust settled, the man heard a distinct *gulp* coming from one of his demon adversaries. The sound didn't surprise him—after all, not many humans could survive the force of a spell that was usually enough to wipe out an entire horde of monsters unscathed all without a single scratch. He could tell that the demons were finally starting to realize what they were up against.

As the demons' eyes fell upon the man's youthful face, they quickly paled with despair. His eyes were the deepest of blacks—as if all the world's darkness had pooled within his irises. The man let out another sigh before lowering his right arm, still tingling a bit from blocking the previous attack.

"Are you trying to *insult* me or is that really the best you can do?" he asked.

"Insult you? God, no. That attack would have wiped any normal human off the face of the planet!" replied the demon.

Spread out across the horizon lay no vast plains or great ocean, but an unending horde of monsters. These were monsters usually seen in only the deepest depths of a labyrinth, most of them several times larger than the man they were united against. The only people to be found were the group of demons standing in a line in front of them—and the lone human man opposing them. It was a state of affairs that would leave most men begging for their lives, and one in which no one would have laughed at the man for discarding his pride and fleeing with his tail between his legs. Yet this man simply stood there, unable to resist the urge to snicker. Many of the demons had taken a few steps back, horrified at what they'd just witnessed.

"You're mad, you know that? You're no human. You're a monster—an abomination!" said the demon, a cold sweat breaking out on his forehead as he watched the young human grin from ear to ear.

The man did not seem offended, and simply nodded in agreement. "Yeah, I bet it probably seems that way from your perspective. But let the record show that it wasn't me who decided you were going to die here by my hand today. *You* were the one who dared to mess around with our fates... Isn't that right, *Abe Mahiro*?" asked the man, deliberately calling out the demon's name in an order customarily used only in another world.

At this, the demon couldn't help but flinch. He knew his back was up against the wall. Then, the human man raised his arm to chest level once more and recited a magical incantation of his own.

"Shadow Magic, activate!"

A deeper darkness than the world had ever known fell over the land. Cries of fear and confusion rang out as the man's enemies were trapped beneath a veil of darkness that left them unable to see who was standing next to them.

"I guess I should probably thank you, though," said the man. "After all, it was you who turned me into the abomination I am today. You, who gave me the strength I'd need to do what needed to be done. But unfortunately for you, that doesn't mean I'll let you off the hook for what you've done."

With that, the man raised both hands toward the heavens as if to beckon them down. "O Lord, let me embody all the multitude of evils that dwell within this world! *Divine Retribution!*"

As soon as the words left the man's lips, the darkness warped and morphed into figures of various shapes and sizes. A moment later, cries of agony and despair rang out from all around.

"Now, may you all be consumed by that which you fear *most*."

In what seemed like only the blink of an eye, the enemy forces were reduced to a single demonic man. All the rest had been devoured without a trace, not even leaving a speck of flesh behind.

And so it was that a battle that should have been a war stacked heavily in the demons' favor was reduced to a one-on-one match between a single demon and an abomination.

My Status *as an*
Assassin *Obviously*
Exceeds *the* Hero's

— ✦ CHAPTER 1 ✦ —

In Vengeance's Wake

POV: AMELIA ROSEQUARTZ

AKIRA RETURNED TO THE HOTEL just as the morning sun was beginning its ascent. I was sitting in my chair in the living room, watching as the sky changed from black to navy before brightening through the entire spectrum of blues. I was sitting there, basking in the shimmering rays as they crept up my face, when suddenly, I gasped as a black silhouette leapt into the room via an open window. I hadn't been able to sleep a wink that night, but when the wave of relief washed over me upon seeing he'd made it home safely, I suddenly felt very drowsy indeed. Crow had long since retired to his bedchambers, but an elderly man like him would probably be awake again before long.

"Akira...!!!"

I ran over to him but stopped short when my nose picked up the heavy stench of blood. I grimaced. Though it was not immediately obvious, his black cloak was stained red with blood—I could tell it was not Akira's, nor was it an amount that could have come from a single victim.

"Sorry," was his first word to me.

Though...I wasn't sure what exactly he was apologizing for. For pretending not to hear me when I begged him not to go? Or for the simple act of slaughtering more people? My emotions ran wild, and soon, I could feel tears running down my cheeks.

"*Why*...? How could you just...?"

As I stuttered through my sobs, Akira ruffled my hair a bit more roughly than usual and then began to explain what happened in a disaffected tone. Apparently, he'd had to kill a fellow assassin—one who'd also been hired to assassinate Gram—before he even made it to his target. He'd apparently felt nothing after doing this—no rush of emotions, no guilt, nor any regret. Akira had his back to the sunlit window, so his face was hidden in shadow: but I could imagine his pained expression.

"Anyway," said Akira, "the fact of the matter is, it was high time I stopped being a sorry excuse for an assassin and lived up to my title. Maybe if I'd done that from the start, Commander Saran wouldn't have had to die like he did."

He was referring to the time when he uncovered the king of Retice's evil plot shortly after being summoned to this world but didn't have the stomach to take him out. But in this world, just because one was an assassin didn't mean they were obligated to assassinate people—in fact, few did. While one's class was assigned at birth and there was nothing anyone could do to change it, that didn't make it an absolute mandate. There were plenty who, like the Ur guildmaster Lingga, were assassins on paper but pursued entirely different lines of work. A majority simply ended up working as adventurers. Yet Akira had apparently decided he was going to be a *true* assassin.

"No, Akira! What happened to the commander wasn't your fault...!"

"Maybe not, but I had the opportunity to kill the king back then, and the only reason I didn't was because I got cold feet. It was my cowardice that got Saran killed."

I shuddered. I had hoped avenging Saran Mithray would finally give Akira the closure he needed to move on, yet the look on his face was far more haggard and distressed than it had been when I sent him into forced sleep. And this time, I didn't think it was the sort of thing any amount of rest could resolve.

More than anything, I wanted to keep Akira's hands clean, though I realized it was just my own selfishness talking. The reality was that Akira was in a lot of pain right now, and I needed to find some way to help him through it. Hastily wiping away my tears with my sleeve, I lifted my head and looked at Akira, who still stood against a backdrop of morning light.

"...Perhaps, but if it hadn't been for that, you and I might never have met," I said. "Why, I could have just been stuck inside of that slime until it sapped every last bit of mana from my body. Then I never would have been able to make up with Kilika, among other things. I know it's easy to get caught up wondering about what-if scenarios, Akira, but at the end of the day...all we can do is live in the present."

All we can do is live in the present.

I had to admit, even I was a little surprised by the words myself. To think that someone like me, who'd once tried so hard to erase her past self and the things she'd done, would ever reach a point where she could try to help someone else avoid making the same mistake, was surprising.

"I won't tell you not to have any regrets, or to try not to think about it too hard," I continued, "but please, don't let it consume your entire identity. More than anything, we need to keep our eyes focused on the road ahead. Don't you agree?"

In the dim, morning light, Akira gently wiped away the tears from my damp cheeks. His hands were shockingly cold, as if he had washed them before he'd returned.

"...I don't have a fraction of your life experience, Amelia, nor will I ever. Human lives just aren't long enough for that. So, it's not that easy for me to just change who I am overnight... But I'll tell you this: I'm terrified of the part of me that can kill a man and think nothing of it. I'm also terrified of the part of me that thinks everything would be better if I'd just murdered the royal family when I had the chance."

I could tell Akira was being completely honest. And it sounded like, as much as he regretted not killing the king of Retice, he also felt profoundly terrified of himself for wishing he had. He was still just a teenage boy, so I could only imagine how unstable his heart and mind were. It hurt to see him trying so desperately to pour his heart out to me. Akira, who had lived his entire short life in a world at peace, and me, who'd lived longer than he could even fathom and had seen many a hellish tragedy in her time. There were so many things between the two of us we couldn't hope for the other to understand, but I still wanted nothing more than for us to be together.

I took a step forward and reached out my hand. "I'm sorry, Akira. I don't know what it is you're afraid of exactly, but I can assure you that you have nothing to fear. At least for as long as Night and I are around," I said, reaching up and pulling his head down to my chest as I sat down on the couch. I ran my fingers through his raven-black hair. He simply let it happen. I whispered softly in his ear, trying my best to give off a tone of motherly affection: "No matter what happens, I'll never stop wanting to be with you, Akira. And I know that Night feels the same. Don't you?"

"...I want to stay with you guys too. No matter what might become of me, I want you to know that will never change," he replied in a hoarse voice, his shoulders trembling ever so slightly beneath his bloodstained cloak. Then he lifted his head and wrapped his arms around me. "Thanks, Amelia. I'm still gonna need some time to get back on my feet after this, but you've definitely cheered me up a little bit."

"I'm just happy to be of help. Now, why don't you go and take a shower?" I asked, patting him on the back and pushing him in the direction of the bathroom. He turned and looked back at me with swollen, red eyes and nodded. And while I was sure he wouldn't appreciate being thought of this way, I couldn't help but marvel at how cute he was when he did what I said.

POV: LIA LAGOON

I F SOMEONE WERE TO ASK ME to make a list of the most unlikely events in the world, Uncle Gram getting murdered would have ranked pretty high on that list.

My uncle was a villain, no two ways about it. He abused his position in the royal family to commit a number of heinous atrocities, and in recent years, his villainy had apparently transcended the boundaries of our nation and made victims of the other races as well. I only said "apparently" because I did not receive the information firsthand, as my uncle did a good job covering his tracks and my adoptive father seems to be complicit. It felt like I was trapped in an inescapable situation; for as long as the king allowed my uncle to commit atrocities unpunished, his crimes would no doubt continue.

I could only assume this was also the reason His Majesty had seen fit to dismantle the public order committee that once existed to prevent such corruption. He was all too happy to let other people take the fall for my uncle's crimes—and line his pockets all the while. As a lowly adopted child, I was in no position to confront him about any of it, and I didn't think there was anyone left in this country who could have put a stop to their machinations. My adoptive father, being the king, was heavily guarded at all times and my uncle, even more so. The idea of someone breaking through such defenses and successfully assassinating either of them seemed like a most fanciful dream.

"...I'm sorry, could you say that one more time?"

"Y-yes, milady. It seems your uncle, the royal prince, has been murdered by an unknown assailant."

When I had noticed a commotion stirring in the castle that morning, I asked my most well-informed lady-in-waiting to look into it, and she discovered that my uncle had been killed.

My most unlikely scenario had come to pass.

"...Who could have done such a thing?"

The only reason I'd been adopted into the royal family was for my rare class: that of Guardian. While traditional barriers could only protect a predetermined point in space, guardians could cast barriers around specific individuals that would move with them, and I was able to sustain the barriers for an almost infinite amount of time, barring any unforeseen circumstances. The royal family had wanted to take advantage of my powers, so my uncle was protected by one of my barriers at all times. In order to kill him, one would need to first break through my barrier—something I could usually immediately sense.

I had sensed no such thing, and when I focused, I found that the Spirit Barrier I had cast on my uncle was still intact.

"And what of his subordinates?" I asked.

"According to my sources, they were all found deceased with stab wounds to their vital organs. It's suspected they were killed by someone other than the prince's murderer, but a skilled assassin, nonetheless."

No kidding, I thought to myself. My uncle's bodyguards were mute but extremely powerful. It would have taken quite the deft hand to kill any of them with a single stab. But more than anything, I was most puzzled by the fact that my uncle's barrier remained intact. My uncle's assassin was skilled enough to have somehow bypassed my barrier and kill him in spite of it—there were scant few people capable of such a feat.

"...No! It can't be!"

"Lady Lia?!"

An assassination technique that could slip through even a powerful barrier... I knew one person who possessed such superhuman abilities. A man who had recently been asked by my adoptive father to assassinate my uncle, no less. A boy from another world who looked to be about the same age as me. The one who I had personally watched send hordes of monsters to their graves in the depths of the labyrinth—the strongest assassin in the entire world, whose physical strength rivaled that of even the demons. And with whom Lord Crow was—

As soon as the realization hit me, I took off running. My attendant called after me, but I paid her no mind and kept sprinting down the corridor. I didn't know what exactly was making me so anxious and impatient, but I knew I needed to see Lord Crow as soon as possible. I could feel in my heart that some sort of permanent change had occurred overnight, and it scared me.

POV: ODA AKIRA

W HEN I AWOKE, the sun was just about to reach its peak overhead. And while I would have certainly said that Uruk, the City of Water, had thus far lived up to its reputation as one of this world's most beautiful and relaxing tourist destinations, the furious screaming that woke me was decidedly neither beautiful nor relaxing.

Ever since my time alone down in the Great Labyrinth of Kantinen, I had learned to control my sleep patterns so I could never be taken by surprise. Yet the reassuring words Amelia had whispered in my ear when I returned at dawn had soothed my heart to such an extent that I fell into an uncharacteristically deep sleep after I'd showered. I hadn't felt so refreshed since the time I fainted from mana exhaustion, or perhaps, since the time Amelia used her magic to put me to sleep.

Hard to believe a few words could have the same effect as her powerful magic.

As I slowly climbed out of bed, I let out a long, hearty yawn. I stretched out my limbs and was surprised to find I was feeling fit as a fiddle. I looked outside and saw the sun's high position— apparently I had slept until almost noon.

Meanwhile, the angry voices in the next room were still going at it. The walls were pretty well soundproofed in this hotel, so I couldn't make out every word, but from what I could gather, Lia had come to the room demanding to see someone and Amelia was being uncharacteristically vehement in her objection. I could hear Crow's voice in the mix as well, so I assumed Lia wasn't here to see him, which meant she probably wanted to talk to me. I was struck by the sudden recollection that the beastman I had killed last night was technically a member of the royal family, so Lia would have probably heard the news sooner than most. I felt a chill run down my spine.

"What's going on out here?" I asked, opening the door to the bedroom. The conversation halted immediately, and Amelia dashed over to me.

"Are you sure you don't need more rest, Akira?"

"I'm fine. Haven't felt this well rested in a good while, actually."

As I watched a wave of relief wash over Amelia's face, I felt terrible for having worried her so much, but before I could say anything else, Lia marched right up to me. She seemed uncharacteristically riled up.

"Lord Akira, I apologize for intruding on you without warning. There's just something I'd like to verify with you," she began.

Yeah, no doubt this is about Gram.

"Am I correct to assume it was you who assassinated my uncle, Guildmaster Gram?"

I could tell immediately she wasn't even considering the possibility it had been someone other than me. She was asking this not as a question but as confirmation. And since it was pointless to lie, I simply nodded in response. "That's right. I was the one who killed him...but don't get the wrong idea. I didn't do it because your old man asked me to. Feel free to tell him I don't need any reward."

I assassinated Gram for Crow and Crow alone—there was no ambiguity in my mind. My statement seemed to confuse Lia, however, as she tilted her head to the side. Presumably, Crow hadn't told her the full story. I shot him a look, as if to ask his permission. There must have been a reason he hadn't told her, perhaps out of concern for her well-being. To my surprise, Crow nodded back, giving his approval, so I took a deep breath and prepared to answer Lia's unspoken question.

"It was Crow who asked me to assassinate Gram, long before your father did, so it took priority. Though that's not to say I didn't have my own reasons for wanting the man dead."

Lia only seemed more confused. Slowly, she turned to face Crow, as if begging for an explanation. Thankfully, he obliged.

"That 'fellow countryman' who killed my sister? That was Gram," Crow announced in a relaxed voice I had never heard from him before.

Apparently, this was all Lia needed to put the pieces together, and her expression turned grim. "Then...that 'innocent kid' you mentioned yesterday...that was Lord Akira? And the 'dirty work' you roped him into...that was *killing* my Uncle Gram?!"

Lia had managed to stay relatively calm up until now, and she was really putting the screws to Crow. Crow, for his part, didn't look too bothered, but I could tell this wasn't his ideal scenario.

"...Fine, so *now* you've had your revenge, even if you had to get someone else to do it for you. So now what are you gonna do with your life, wise guy?!" Lia pressed, the heartbreak palpable in her voice.

Off to the side, I saw Amelia grimace. Lia was like something of a second sister to her, so it didn't surprise me that she was highly sympathetic to her pain.

"...For now, I have to hold up my end of the bargain with Akira. Once that's done... Well, I honestly don't know what I'll do with myself," Crow replied. His motivation in life up until now had been to exact revenge on his sister's murderer: to kill Gram. Now that that was done, what was there left for him to do? I had a few ideas, though...none of them were particularly pleasant.

"Did you know all along that things were going to end up like this, Lord Akira?" Lia asked, her head hung low.

I shook my head. I had my own beef with Gram over Commander Saran's murder, and while I certainly didn't usually see myself as judge, jury, and executioner, I had made my own judgment that Gram was the sort of villain who didn't deserve to live. Not to imply I had the right to decide who lived and who died, but I knew that the loved ones of Gram's victims wouldn't be able to move on until he was dead and buried. So, despite my misgivings, I made the tough call to follow through with Crow's request, not out of any sense of obligation but through my own judgment.

After staring at the ground for a good while, Lia quickly raised her head as though she'd made up her mind about something. "Lord Akira...no, Lord Crow—I've decided I'm coming with you as well!" she declared.

"Whoa, whoa, *whoa*! Do you have any idea what you're signing up for?!" Crow shot back in an unusual display of anger. I wasn't sure I'd ever seen him so agitated before. Hell, I didn't think I'd ever heard him raise his voice.

"Of course I do! You all are about to set off for the demon continent, correct?" Lia asked, looking to me for confirmation. I nodded, and Crow gave me a dirty look that I tried my best to ignore. No doubt he simply didn't want to put his sweet little Lia in danger. "Then I'm sure there'll come a time when my barriers will come in handy, *right*?! You have to take me with you!"

I could only assume Lia was using her barriers as an excuse, but it wasn't long before even Crow had to nod in approval under the fierce determination in her eyes. Amelia broke into a huge grin, and I couldn't help but wonder what was going through her mind.

"Okay, we're heading out!"

After Crow explained to Lia that we had no further business in Uruk now that Gram was dead, she made a quick trip back to the palace to gather her things and meet us at the edge of the city. When we got there, we found her waiting for us, accompanied by more luggage than any one person could ever need. She probably tried to beat us because she suspected Crow would try to leave without her.

"Don't think you're the only one who knows his way around town, Lord Crow! I've lived here long enough to know a good shortcut or two, and I—"

"Why are you here?" Crow interrupted Lia's cutesy braggadocio in a cold, monotone voice, almost too quiet to hear. You could have cut the tension in the air with a knife. The utter lack of malice in his voice almost made it *more* intimidating.

"When I said I was coming along with you earlier, you gave your approval. You didn't tell me where exactly we were meeting up, though, so I had to make a wild guess and beat you to the punch. But that's okay. There's no home left for me here anymore."

Lia seemed awfully proud of herself, but if she was really so good at predicting Crow's actions, why did it seem like she couldn't tell he was so clearly pissed off? Or maybe she did know and was agitating him on purpose. Though I had to wonder what she meant by there being no home for her in Uruk anymore. I had a hard time imagining the greedy king ever letting someone with powers like hers go so easily.

"I dunno what you think the demon continent's gonna be like, but I can promise you it's at least a few hundred times more dangerous than the pleasure cruise you're envisioning," Crow snarled. "It sure as hell ain't no place for a pampered royal like you!"

"Don't worry about me! I'll be fine!" Lia replied with an energetic nod. "I'm not as weak as you think I am! And I've already cut all ties with the royal family. I'm just Lia now, not Lia Lagoon."

"...So I see."

How the hell did she cut ties with the royal family that fast? I wondered, but Amelia quickly took the words right out of my mouth.

"I have a hard time believing the royal family would give up its precious adopted daughter so easily. How'd you pull that off?" she asked.

"It was simple, really. They only cared about my barriers, not me. I just had to promise to keep my barriers cast over the palace and the king after leaving the royal family. Though I only made that promise to the *current* king, so all bets are off if he has to step down for any unforeseen reason." Lia smirked like a child who'd just played a cruel prank and gotten away with it. I was a little taken aback; she seemed much more animated now than she had been during her time in the royal family. I could only assume we were finally seeing her true self.

"A wise choice. Now that Gram's been assassinated, there's no doubt gonna be plenty of scandalous information that comes to light, which won't reflect kindly on the royal family. Gram did an awful lot to help conceal the corrupt ways of the royal family and the upper nobility in exchange for them turning a blind eye to his crimes."

Figures. I'd had nothing but bad experiences with royal families in this world, with maybe the *only* exception being the elven royal family. Still, Victor and the other castle guards seemed like good people, even if they were a little too hotheaded for their own good.

Crow whirled around and started walking, his back to Lia. "More than anything," Crow began, "the people are quickly gonna find out that the king was complicit in Gram's human trafficking and slavery, and we all know how beastfolk feel about those two things. I leaked the information about it myself. Won't be long before the citizens try to storm the castle, I'm guessing."

...Wait a minute. And your plan was to just leave Lia there to suffer through all of that?

Lia seemed to come to the same conclusion, as I noticed her shoulders were trembling as she hung her head. But knowing Crow, surely he'd had some strategic arrangement in place to make sure Lia was safe. He loved to act cold and unfeeling, but when it came to her, he was a real softie at heart.

"...Now, c'mon, we'd better hit the road," Crow said.

"Oh, no you don't!" Lia growled, her mouth curling into a frown. "You can't just drop a plot bomb like that and not explain yourself! Get back here, Lord Crow!"

POV: SATOU TSUKASA

I T ALL started a few days ago.

After leaving the city of Uruk ahead of the others and making our way toward the rendezvous point at the tip of the beastfolk domain closest to the demon continent, Gilles, myself, and the other heroes found ourselves in a dire spot of trouble.

"...Ugh, I'm so huuuuuuuungryyy..."

"Can it, Ueno! You're just gonna make the rest of us even *hungrier!*"

That's right: we were all out of food.

Our party had been moving from town to town thus far, so as long as we had money, we were never too far from our next meal. And even if we didn't, most guild branches had plenty of monster-slaying quests available, so it was easy enough to make the money to stave off starvation. But now, we were making our way through a dense forest, with no towns up ahead—and the monsters we were encountering were only growing stronger. It took a lot of stamina to weave through the trees with such poor footing, so we had expended our food supply in no time flat.

We needed to solve our impending hunger crisis ASAP.

"Well, I certainly wasn't expecting there to be so few animals out here," I said with a sigh as I scanned the area. According to Gilles, the people from the nearby villages called this the "Forest of Demise," and it was deeply feared because, supposedly, any who dared to enter it would be attacked by terrifying beasts...and never return. To be fair, the powerful monsters we'd seen did lend some credence to the stories. Certainly, an average person would be better off staying away from the forest rather than testing their luck.

Physically, my stats had come a long way since we first arrived in this world, and my senses were more acute too. I was able to tell the difference between a simple animal and a monster by scent alone, though right now, I could tell that there were neither animals nor monsters within a twenty-meter radius of our position. Nor were there any birds flying through the sky in this neck of the woods.

Apparently, the monsters that lay in wait up ahead were just *that* fearsome. And it was our job to take them out before Akira and the others got here... Though I was pretty sure he and Amelia could handle anything this forest might throw at them with their eyes closed.

As I pictured this in my head, I couldn't help but snicker. It was hard to believe how completely my opinion of Akira had changed since being summoned to Morrigan. It probably had a lot to do with what had happened during our first trip down into the labyrinth, and when he was forced to flee the castle. How was I not supposed to respect him after all of that?

"Hey! Whatcha laughin' for, Tsukasa? This ain't no joke! We're all gonna starve to death at this rate!"

I apologized to Ueno, who was angrily glaring at me, and started trying to think of a solution to our predicament. We knew there was a river with clear, drinkable water nearby. All we needed was a source of food, preferably something we could preserve or that wouldn't spoil as we carried it along with us.

"Okay, let's all spread out in different directions, gather up anything that looks edible, and then meet back here. We don't want anyone to get into any trouble without backup, though, so let's go in groups of two or three. Leave marks on the trees so you can find your way back, and don't wander off on your own under any circumstances."

The groups we ultimately decided upon were me, Ueno, and Tsuda; Asahina, Waki, and Hosoyama; and lastly, Gilles and Nanase. Each group headed off in different directions from the clearing we'd chosen as base camp. As long as we kept track of which way we'd gone, we'd be able to make our way back. I looked at Gilles to make sure he was okay with this plan, and while he did look a bit conflicted, he ultimately gave his approval.

"Okay, once the sun reaches its highest point in the sky, let's all agree to start heading back here. Now, off you go, everyone!"

To be honest, I didn't think it was a very good idea to be splitting up in dangerous territory, even in groups of two or three, but at least we weren't going to be going very far. And with myself, Asahina, and Gilles spread across each of the three teams, we should be able to handle any monsters we might encounter.

Everything should be just fine.

Looking back on it, I think there must have been something wrong with my head. Otherwise, I couldn't guess why I would have ever thought it was a good idea to split up and head into completely unknown territory.

POV: ASAHINA KYOUSUKE

HAVING BEEN ASSIGNED BY SATOU to a team with Waki and Hosoyama, I immediately began surveying the vicinity for possible foodstuffs. The trees were so tall, you couldn't see the tops of them, and their trunks were all so massive it would take more than the three of us to link arms around even the *smallest*. I wondered how old the trees were and marveled at how many wars and dynasties they must have lived through.

These were the thoughts that ran through my mind as I made my way silently through the trees, cutting marks into each trunk as we went to indicate the way back. Waki had instructed his tamed animal companions to search the surrounding area for food while Hosoyama was searching through the various grasses on the ground in the hopes of finding something edible. My intended role was, I presumed, to serve as their guard. I stood at the ready, prepared to counter any threats that might ambush us.

However, I had to wonder if there was some ill will behind the team assignments. While neither Waki nor Hosoyama was a social butterfly by any means, I was fairly certain I'd never seen them exchange a single word with one another. I could only assume Satou had, for whatever reason, put us into groups with people he knew would have a harder time getting along.

"Oh, hey! You find something up there, little fella?" Waki asked one of his tamed animals as it clambered down a tree with some fruit in its mouth. As he gave it some scritches and held it in his arms, it was clear the animal had taken quite the liking to Waki—especially compared to how it had only growled at him at first. For more and more animals to grow attached to him so easily meant he'd raised his level as an animal trainer significantly. Apparently, the oafish boy had been putting in quite a bit of work on his own time.

"Hey, Hosoyama! Take a look at these. You think they're cherries?" Waki called, holding out the fruits of his pet's labor. They were indeed shaped like cherries, though the bulbs on the end of each stem were closer to the size of peaches.

Hosoyama, our resident healer, was highly attuned to whether things contained poison or not. If her analysis said that they were edible, then chances were, they were safe to eat. "Cherries? I dunno. Let's have a taste."

"H-hey!"

But before Waki could protest, she'd already popped one into her mouth as though it was nothing, despite the worry painted clearly on both of our faces. I let out a relieved sigh upon seeing that she did not immediately keel over dead.

"What the heck were you *thinking*?! That could've been poisonous, y'know!" Waki cried, hoarsely.

I had to agree it seemed more than a little careless on Hosoyama's part, but she simply grinned from ear to ear. "Aw, it's fine. Healers have a skill that negates any hazardous substances we might ingest into our bodies, silly. Though...I only learned about it a little while ago, tee hee."

In other words, poison would have no effect on her. This knowledge made me a lot more hopeful about our chances of surviving our current predicament. Once we reconvened with the others, she could serve as the poison tester for any foods the other groups might bring back.

"Sorry for not telling you guys sooner. I wasn't sure how well the skill would work because I hadn't had a chance to try it out yet," she went on with a smile.

A chill ran down my spine. *This girl has nerves of steel!*

"Anyway, I'm happy to taste test any and all foods you guys might find. Oh, and these 'cherries' of yours taste more like peaches, and they're *super* delicious! The skin's a little bitter, though, so I might recommend peelin' 'em first."

"Got it! Thanks for your services, Hosoyama!"

In the end, thanks to Hosoyama's poison-testing abilities, our group was able to gather a wide variety of different tree fruits. With all this fruit, our entire group would be able to eat pretty decently.

"Looks like the sun's about to reach the top of the sky. Let's head back!"

We'd moved in a fairly straight line, so all we really had to do was turn around and walk back. Feeling rather pleased with ourselves, we followed the marks I'd left on the trees and hurried back to the rendezvous point.

"What the...?" said Waki, who had taken point. Eventually, we reached the last of the marks I'd left on the trees. But the small clearing we'd set as our rendezvous point was nowhere to be seen.

POV: NANASE RINTAROU

I THINK THE FIRST PERSON to notice something fishy was going on wasn't Gilles, Tsukasa, or Kyousuke: it was me. I didn't know it then, but I later learned that, at a certain point in their development, wind mages acquire the subconscious ability to "read the wind," as it was commonly referred to. Similar to a hunch or premonition, this innate skill allowed a person to intuitively sense when they were approaching a potentially dangerous situation.

"Something seems quite off about this forest, don't you think?" I asked Gilles.

I'd had a funny feeling since we'd entered the woods and noticed none of the others seemed to suspect anything was off. It was so disconcerting for me that I couldn't shrug it off as mere paranoia, so I wanted Gilles's opinion on the matter. Thankfully, I'd been placed in a group alone with him, but I was evidently too late in bringing it up.

"Nanase, on your guard. I'm sensing hostiles, though they're still a ways off. We're being surrounded," he warned me in a low voice after scanning the vicinity for food.

The thought of being surrounded by enemies in unfamiliar territory made my entire body seize up. Being a wind mage, I'd always supported the group from the rear, no matter how much I'd wished I could have fought on the front line. I'd never had to face an attack head-on. It had mostly been up to Tsukasa and Kyousuke to hold the line. We hadn't faced any monsters strong enough to break through a hero and a samurai, so I had never been in such danger before. I was unsure how to handle an enemy charging straight for my throat.

"*Eep!!!*"

When I felt a hand touch my shoulder, I nearly jumped out of my boots, thinking an ambush was already upon me. But it was only Gilles, though the expression on his face was far grimmer than I was used to. He squeezed my shoulder tightly.

"Be calm. Unless you want to die here, you need to focus on your own survival *right now* and be prepared to do whatever it takes to stay alive," he ordered before stepping in front of me, drawing his blade, and bracing for imminent combat. From that vantage point, his frame seemed a lot bigger, his shoulders a lot broader than ever before. "Now, listen to me so we can survive! I'll get us through this!"

His words snapped me out of my anxiety, and I clenched my fists. This was not the disaffected, formal tone of the Gilles I thought I knew—this was the voice of a man who felt more than a little frantic, and it hit me like a ton of bricks. I wasn't strong enough to survive on my own like Akira could, and I didn't have Tsukasa's charisma to make everyone else band together either. Unlike Kyousuke, I also had no specialties; and I couldn't cook nor was I the life of the party. I couldn't even reassure others when they were feeling down.

I didn't have any unique skills to speak of.

But I still wanted to survive. I wasn't ready to die… I wanted to make it back home, just like the rest of my classmates. I wanted to wake up and get scolded by my parents for sleeping in. I wanted to rush all the way to school, screw around with my friends, study hard, eat lunch, and live out my boring ordinary life the same way I always had. But in order to do that, I had to *fight*. Maybe the threat of being attacked had shocked me back into a state of alertness, because my frozen hands were brimming with warmth again.

I'd finally found the resolve I needed to fight and survive in this world—something Akira had probably done the very first day we arrived here. I would no longer simply go along with what others decided. I was going to live by my own will.

"Yes, sir!!!" I cried. "I'll do whatever it takes not to die! So please, sir, tell me what you need me to do! What do I have to do to make it out of this alive?" I raised my head, gripping my staff tightly, and looked Gilles directly in the eye.

His eyes widened at my sudden shift in countenance, and he smiled broadly. "Now that's more like it. You need to..."

Gilles whispered instructions in my ear, and I nodded. It wasn't something I'd ever attempted before, but one of the wind mage rules of thumb was that when it came to casting spells, sometimes powerful emotions could be converted directly into tangible strength. Now that I'd found an internal source of determination and will, I was sure I could pull it off.

"Are you ready?"

"Yep, I'm all set!"

I was fully braced to repel the enemy. It felt like it took an awful long time to set up, but, somehow, they still hadn't reached us. I had to wonder if Gilles's enemy-sensing abilities were a bit too sensitive. Granted, that was probably necessary for someone who had been the vice commander of an entire nation's knights, but in my estimation, his effective sensing range was nearly twice that of our hero, Tsukasa, and five times that of Kyousuke. Maybe it was a trait unique to the knight class.

I couldn't help but smile and shake my head at this thought—now that I'd found my resolve, I realized just how little we knew about this world and how many things I'd never questioned. After about a minute, though it felt more like an hour, the enemy drew near enough to see. The tawny brown and green monsters filled my field of vision, then tightened their encirclement one step at a time.

"Are those *trees*?!" I gasped.

"Technically, they're tree monsters known as treants. Generally, they're quite docile, camouflaging themselves as normal trees most of the time...except when they feel threatened or when mating season rolls around," Gilles explained.

Apparently, we'd stumbled into the area at the height of mating season, Gilles told me as he watched the treants slowly make their way into the traps we'd set. I was a little surprised to learn monsters had mating seasons just like other animals and was beginning to wonder whether the distinction between monster and animal was much more arbitrary than I'd originally thought.

The "traps" we'd devised were little more than simple pitfalls—I'd used my wind magic to dig a number of holes around myself and Gilles, each about as deep as an adult male is tall. We hadn't had time to cover the holes with leaves, or fill them with snakes, so they were less pitfalls and more just plain old *pits*. Something with human-level intelligence would have noticed them right away and walked around or jumped over them, but the treants were walking right into them; they weren't the smartest of monsters. Knowledge truly was power, and I was beginning to regret never setting foot in the Retice Castle archives.

"Treants may not be the most intelligent of creatures, but they're no fools either," Gilles warned. "Stay on your guard. I'll keep watching your back, but I need you to remain vigilant. Do you remember the support spells I taught you?"

I nodded.

"Good. Then it's time to put them to the test. Having traveled with your party for some time now, you seem to have a more watchful eye than the rest. I'll be counting on you to look out for me."

I nodded at Gilles's words of encouragement, then held up my staff and said: "I give unto thee the power to slay dragons and to smite even the mightiest of foes! Until my mana is spent, let mine strength be thine... Wind Enchantment: Haste!"

W~ green light.

I took a deep breath, then gathered my mana to begin casting again. "I give unto thee the fortitude to withstand all manner of attacks. Until my mana is spent, let my strength be thine... Wind Enchantment: Barricade!"

After successfully casting two buffs simultaneously, I felt the strength begin to drain from my body. Gilles, once both spells had taken effect, turned and gave me a pat on the head. "Well done. Now you just take it easy and leave the rest to me."

His calm and collected voice helped soothe my mind even as the monsters rapidly closed in on us, but the fatigue from keeping multiple spells active at once was too great. Gilles's voice moved farther and farther away, until, finally, I lost consciousness.

POV: TSUDA TOMOYA

I'D ALWAYS BEEN A WEAKLING—more so mentally than physically. Perhaps the best way to describe me was as a "nervous wreck." There was nothing that terrified me more than having to interact with other humans, and there was nothing I hated more than myself. Every day, I tried my best to act as masculine as I could, but I'd long since grown accustomed to people mistaking me for a girl when meeting me for the first time. I wasn't happy about it, but it was what it was.

But there was someone I aspired to be—almost to the point of obsession (which was seen as a little weird, since we were both guys). *He* was one of my fellow classmates and the star member of our kendo team—Asahina Kyousuke. The first time I laid eyes on him was back in junior high when the various school clubs tried to pull in new recruits. Being the way I was, I found it impossible to say no, so despite having zero experience in kendo, I ended up on the team. I'd hated being such a nervous wreck even then, and I wanted to find a way to fix myself if I could. I thought that by forcing myself to participate in sports or martial arts, I might be able to find the self-confidence to "grow out of it," though you can probably guess how well that went.

Luckily for me, the junior high kendo team wasn't exactly a force to be reckoned with. The only person with even a modicum of experience was one of the girls who'd done some kendo in elementary school, which meant a shrimp like me was able to keep pace with the lessons and drills. Because there weren't many people on the team, by the fall of my first year, I was entered into my first official meet.

As vice-captain of my school's team, my first bout was against a first-year boy who'd spent the morning wiping the floor with all of our third years during the singles round. It was my first real duel, and the cheering that echoed throughout the gymnasium had me quaking in my boots; I kept my eyes closed for most of the match. It wasn't until one of the upperclassmen tried to cheer me up after the fact that I learned my opponent had won—that boy was Asahina.

It should have come as no surprise that a boy with several tournaments under his belt would make short work of an absolute beginner like me, but he managed to land two clean hits and disqualify me in less than ten seconds. The match was over in a flash. Next thing I knew, I was bowing to my opponent before leaving the ring and taking my place at the side of my teammate (who had also quickly lost his own match). Unable to score a single point, our school suffered a crushing defeat and was eliminated from the competition.

We didn't even have time to lament our loss before the next match was scheduled to begin, so we hurriedly gathered our gear, and as we were about to make our exit, one of the alternates on Asahina's team walked up to us and scoffed.

"Was that supposed to be some kinda *joke*? Maybe you guys would be better off entering in the elementary school tournament!"

That was the first time in my entire life I got angry enough to see red. Even the upperclassman beside me was ashamed. But I didn't say a word. I was utterly incensed, but my nervous personality pumped the brakes, and in the end, I wasn't even able to attempt a half-hearted comeback. Feeling powerless, I hung my head in shame.

But then a retort came from a very unexpected source.

"Or perhaps *you* should go fight against elementary schoolers, given your maturity level. I believe there's a children's dojo just down the street. I'd be more than happy to file your club resignation paperwork for you."

My jaw dropped, as did the jaws of my upperclassmen and the alternate who'd insulted us. The boy who'd spoken simply looked at his alternate, straight-faced, as though he'd said exactly what needed to be said. For me, it would have taken an awful lot of courage to speak my mind like that, especially when it was likely to upset the other person. I didn't know if it was any easier for other people, and Asahina probably thought nothing of the exchange, but it showed me just how cool he was.

From that point on, Asahina became my idol. Despite going to a completely different school, I'd still watch him from afar during tournaments. People liked to say there were two possible responses when someone else possessed something they lacked: jealousy or admiration. I decidedly fell into the latter camp. I wanted to be able to speak my mind confidently like Asahina, wanted to be a real man like he was. I knew it was presumptuous to think I could ever be as strong, but I just couldn't help wanting to be *just* like Asahina.

Granted, the simple act of aspiring to be like him never helped fix any of my shortcomings, and before I knew it, we were at the same high school on the same kendo team. As Asahina had won nationals before, I assumed he would be scouted by a school with a more prestigious kendo team, so when I discovered he was going to the same school as me, I was surprised. I later heard through the grapevine that he had turned down every offer he received because they were all too far from home. I was so grateful to my junior high school homeroom teacher for recommending this high school to me. I couldn't understand a word of his math lectures, but when it came to picking out high schools, he was second to none!

I continued looking up to Asahina. Well, maybe not to his ability to step on conversational land mines by prodding at sore subjects whenever he spoke to anyone, though I still envied how easily he spoke to people. However, ever since we arrived in Morrigan, I felt like the gap between me and him was only growing wider. The way I trembled in fear whenever a battle was afoot meant I often ended up back with the rear guard, even though I was a knight. Worse, I hadn't faced a monster head-on since that first trip into the Great Labyrinth of Kantinen.

I hadn't exactly been making an effort to contribute either. I went on and on about how badly I wanted to fix my weakest aspects, but I hadn't made a lick of progress since junior high. In fact, I'd gotten lazy since we arrived in this world and was happy to let Satou and Asahina do all the heavy lifting.

Which was why our current predicament posed such a dilemma for me.

"No, Satou! Hold still, gosh darnit! Yer just gonna reopen yer wounds!"

I was the only one of our group still standing. Satou had been knocked unconscious but was still trying to get back up and defend us despite his injuries. Ueno was trying her hardest to keep him on the ground—she'd suffered a pretty gnarly leg injury herself, so we couldn't run away. The shield I'd been carrying had been smashed to pieces only minutes before. The monsters were closing in, and we were sitting ducks.

Thinking back, Satou had been acting strangely today. His rationale for having us split into teams made sense to me, but it still felt like an odd decision coming from a worrywart like him who wouldn't even have us cross the street without looking both ways a dozen times. Maybe his behavior had something to do with how horribly things had gone during our first trip into the labyrinth, because now he tried to only fight monsters when we had a clear advantage, and he was always exceedingly concerned about negative status effects like curses.

He'd always struck me as a bit unapproachable back at school, but here, he was always thinking of everyone else first and foremost and did everything he could for the party. I hadn't exchanged more than a few words with him, and even I could tell that much, so I found it hard to believe he would ever tell us to split up in such dangerous territory.

My mind floated back to the curse placed upon him in the labyrinth. Ueno had claimed the curse was broken, but as her class level had still been quite low, it was possible it hadn't been completely dispelled and she couldn't tell. Either that, or Satou had been afflicted by a new curse, but we hadn't encountered any shady individuals recently, so the former seemed more likely.

Regardless, we were caught between a rock and a hard place. The tree monsters I had no hope of slaying were closing in, my shield had been destroyed, and the sword in my hand was trembling. I couldn't even step back because my injured comrades were on the ground behind me. The last thing I wanted was to die while still being a pathetic loser who hated himself. I needed to figure out some way to turn this situation around, even though we were at a clear disadvantage, based on our numbers and abilities.

Think, Tomoya, think. What would Asahina do? He was like the ideal protagonist of any adventure novel, so surely he'd keep his cool and just do what needed to be done. Which meant I just needed to fortify myself and do whatever I could.

"H-hey, Ueno!!!" I yelled, my voice shaking with fear.

"Y-yeah, what's up?!" she called back, clearly startled. I couldn't blame her for being surprised as I rarely ever addressed her directly. Still, she didn't have to sound *so* surprised; I wasn't a *total* loser. But the fact that I still had the capacity to think about trivial things helped me calm down a bit.

"Sorry, but I don't think I have what it takes to handle these guys all by myself," I said. "At this rate, the three of us are gonna die here."

I heard them both gulp. They knew there was no way we could run, so the best I could hope to do was hold them off for a bit.

"Fortunately, it seems they've decided we'll be easy targets, so I think they're taking their sweet time to torment us. Which means we still have some time."

"How the heck is that *fortunate*?! Wait... You ain't about to suggest that we just leave Tsukasa and hightail it outta here, are ya?"

I couldn't help but laugh at the notion. Abandoning Satou would probably be the worst possible move. If he died, we'd all be in *deep* trouble. "Of course not! But I don't have the strength to defeat them, which means if any of us are gonna take them down, it'll have to be Satou."

He had managed to remain standing to try to protect us down in the labyrinth for a good long while, even after suffering grievous wounds. And now he was even trying to pick himself up despite fighting off unconsciousness. I felt awful for trying to put him to work in his current condition, but I pulled a glass bottle out from my bag and tossed it over to Ueno regardless.

"W-wait, is this?!" She gulped, cradling the phial in her hands.

Surely Ueno recognized the healing potions they'd provided us all with as we were heading to the labyrinth. Most of my classmates had used their allotment of five up during that same trip, as we had no idea the potions were far outside the average adventurer's price range. I had a feeling this was probably the last one in our possession. We knew how effective they were, and I had every confidence the potion would be able to heal Satou's wounds.

"I'd like you to use Disenchant on him as well, just for good measure. You've noticed how strangely he's been acting today too, haven't you?" I asked. The more I thought about his decision to divide us up, the more it seemed like the sort of blunder Satou would have never made had he been in his right mind.

"A-all right," she said and presumably nodded (she was behind me, so I couldn't see her face). "O baleful curse, return from whence thou came! Disenchant!"

The fact that Ueno's incantation was significantly more succinct compared to how long-winded it was back in the Great Labyrinth of Kantinen was a testament to her growth. When magic users raised their class and skill levels, their incantations shortened, until eventually they gained the ability to cast spells without having to recite anything at all. And while casters like Nanase and Hosoyama had widely versatile spells that could be used for virtually any request, disenchanting magic had decidedly fewer applications and thus was much more difficult to level up.

"Okay, Tsuda! I've disenchanted him!" she yelled.

"Great. I'll buy us some time until he's had a chance to fully recover. Keep an eye on him for me," I said before dashing off with sword in hand.

Despite my experience with kendo, my Swordsmanship skill level wasn't particularly high. If anything, my time on the kendo team had taught me some bad habits that were unnecessary for general sword use—habits that had taken a long time to rectify through training. I was still doing practice swings every day to try to remember what they'd taught us back at the castle, but I wasn't sure if it was helping much.

As one of the tree monsters lashed out at me with its whip-like branches, I dodged to the side and swung my sword. My attack landed, but it wasn't successful in severing the branch, merely scratching the bark. Until now, I'd essentially given up on my attacks being of any use against our enemies. But I could feel myself starting to become a different me.

"Hang in there, Tsuda! Tsukasa's almost healed!"

"Got it!"

I dodged and weaved through the branches as they came at me from the left and right. But my reflexes simply weren't good enough to dodge every attack, so several of their lashes hit their mark.

"*Grrragh!!!*" I grunted after being slapped away like a bug by the most recent attack. I could feel my consciousness beginning to fade as a sharp pain coursed through my back.

"There ya go, Tsuda! He's all fixed up!"

Ueno's words gave me the strength to pick myself back up. I looked over, and there by her side was Satou, who had only moments ago been too gravely injured to even stand.

"Ueno, Tsuda, sorry for conking out on you like that. Just leave the rest to me," he said with a guilty frown before drawing his sword.

I let out an amused laugh. "Don't worry about it! If anything, I feel bad for asking you to take care of these guys right after you were just healed. But yeah, I'll leave the rest to you," I said as I dragged my aching body back to Ueno. When I passed by Satou, he gave me a confident nod, which came as such a relief that I lost my grip on consciousness and was quickly enveloped by the darkness.

CHAPTER 2

Changes

POV: ASAHINA KYOUSUKE

"**W**HAT IS THE MEANING OF THIS?" I whispered after arriving at our supposed destination and looking around. The marks I'd left on the trunks of the trees hadn't changed. Even without them, I remembered the unique characteristics of many of the trees we'd passed, so I knew we'd returned along the same path, but the clearing was nowhere to be seen.

"H-hey, what's going on?!" yelled Waki, frantically looking around. "This isn't the rendezvous point! You tricked us, Asahina!!!"

Waki was leading the pack, so he should have known better than anyone that we'd followed the markings to a T. He was probably lashing out because he was flustered and anxious. But getting flustered in a situation like this could have lethal consequences. As I carefully watched our surroundings, I drew my white katana—the Hakuryuu—from its sheath.

"Calm down, Waki. We're surrounded," warned Hosoyama quietly, just as Waki was about to start wailing again. I was impressed Hosoyama had noticed we were being encircled. Her senses must have been more attuned than I gave her credit for. First her poison testing skills, now this—she was a girl of many hidden talents.

"On your guard, both of you. Stay near me," I said, scanning right and left. There was an unfamiliar and unexpected scent of death in the air. This could turn very bad, very fast.

"Here they come!"

As soon as I heard Hosoyama's cry, I brandished my blade. The monsters were moving so fast my eyes could barely keep up with them. It would be difficult for me to fend them off while protecting my companions. I couldn't make out what the enemies looked like, though their arms looked more like branches, so it was easy to assume they were some kind of tree monster.

"...I don't do well with having to fight and protect at the same time," I whispered low enough that my companions couldn't hear. My class was Samurai, not Knight. My specialty was cleaving foes in two, not defending the weak. As such, my defense stat was fairly low, and it usually fell to Tsuda or Nanase to keep the rear fighters safe while Satou and I focused on taking out the enemies. With no Tsuda in sight, the only person around to protect Waki and Hosoyama...was me.

"They should be coming into view any second now..." murmured Hosoyama.

It was strange—we could all sense their malice coming closer and closer, yet we still couldn't see what they really looked like. *Wait a minute. Could it be...*

"Watch out!" I cried, whirling around and cutting straight through the tree monster that had snuck up behind my companions. Its branches were mere inches from the two of them. "They're tree monsters! Be on the lookout for their branches!"

I'd identified our assailants, but we were already surrounded, and it was nearly impossible to tell the monsters apart from the real thing. Trying to feel their respective presences didn't work either since they had us surrounded.

"We have no choice. I'll just have to cut down each and every one."

I drew my second katana from its sheath at my waist. This was the blade they had given me when I first learned my class back at Retice Castle. With one blade in each hand, I was able to make use of my *Dual Blades* skill. It was something I'd practiced in private night after night but still hadn't mastered. It was decidedly more difficult than simply wielding one sword with both hands, and you had to give up on defense and focus on taking the enemy out before they could hit you.

"Psst! I know this probably isn't the time or place, but do you remember Asahina ever being this bullheaded before?"

"H-how should I know?!"

I could hear my companions talking behind me, but I was too focused on the battle to listen.

"Dual Blade Technique: Sakura Tempest!"

This was a skill that sliced indiscriminately in every direction and from every angle, like falling cherry blossoms picked up by a mighty gusting gale. Yet even this would not be strong enough to cut these foes to their cores. I could hear the monsters bellowing in pain from having their branches cut, which meant it was time to deal the decisive blow.

"Dual Blade Technique: Blade Whirlwind!!!"

A gust of wind blew through the area. I could hear Hosoyama squeal, and Waki wailed in surprise behind me. When the wind died down, all that remained were severed trunks of trees all around us and no signs of life to be found. I had successfully dispatched each and every one of them.

I let out a sigh and sheathed my blades.

"That was *wild*, Asahina!"

I turned around to find both Waki and Hosoyama still standing, neither of them having suffered any harm. Still, the attack had served as a sobering reminder of how dangerous uncharted territory could be and that there was no way the old me could have possibly made it out of the situation unscathed. I took a moment to acknowledge just how much stronger I'd become since leaving the castle.

"Sorry for suspecting you earlier," Waki went on. "I should know better than to think you'd ever deceive us. I guess I wasn't thinking straight."

"It's fine. You were caught up in the heat of the moment. Anyone would lose their cool in a situation like that."

Waki certainly wasn't the deepest thinker of the group, but at least he knew how to apologize and own up to his mistakes. Being able to unreluctantly admit one's faults was an important skill, and I admired him for that. Most of my classmates and I had rarely shared any interactions before we were summoned to

Morrigan, but now I was finally getting to know their respective strengths and weaknesses.

"So, what do we do now? I'm guessing those marks we left were all on those tree monsters, so now we have no way of regaining our bearings," Hosoyama said.

I scanned the immediate vicinity. "...It looks like we may still be in luck," I said.

POV: NANASE RINTAROU

B Y THE TIME I WOKE UP, about an hour had passed. After assuring Gilles I didn't need any more rest, I sat up. My body felt heavy and tired. Casting not one but two new enchantment spells at the same time had taken more mental energy than anything I'd done in my short life. I had a major headache too. I'd never even focused that hard during a heated gaming session before.

"It's probably because you tried using spells outside your wheelhouse. Sorry, I shouldn't have pushed you like that," Gilles said, clearly feeling more than a little guilty.

Enchantments were a type of magic that were only effective when placed on someone other than the caster. They used a type of mana different from what was used in attack spells, which meant only certain people could use them at all. I'd only used attack spells before today—the support spells had hit me like a bolt of lightning.

I should have expected as much, really; video games always had power-up and speed-up spells, and there was no reason for this world to be any different. Since I generally played a tank-type character, I only ever focused on attacking. The existence of support spells had slipped my mind.

Part of me wondered if one reason Gilles had taught me those support spells was because he felt like my magical repertoire was lacking, but it was also clear he wanted me to buff him to ensure his own stamina and mana wouldn't run out. And I couldn't really blame him—after all, I often sacrificed my weaker characters to ensure my main powerhouse could survive too.

"Those monsters attacked us like an organized group, wouldn't you say?" I wondered aloud. "Which means it's likely other groups of them are not too far from here."

Treants didn't strike me as migratory creatures, so I could only assume we were trespassing on their home turf. Something told me they'd been waiting for us to split up so we'd be easier to pick off; we had to be playing right into the enemy's hands. I expressed this line of thought to Gilles, whose eyes went wide as he let out an awkward laugh.

"You heroes, I swear. You and Akira share an awfully unique way of analyzing things."

Now it was my turn to laugh awkwardly. "Well, he and I *do* like a lot of the same genres, so I guess that makes sense. There's a form of entertainment back in our world that requires some tactical knowledge, albeit not to the extent a solider like you would have, obviously. But that's where Akira and I are coming from. I'm sure if you asked someone like Kyousuke, though, he'd give you a different answer entirely."

"A 'form of entertainment,' you say..." Gilles muttered under his breath.

I could totally understand why someone in his position would have a hard time seeing tactical warfare as entertainment. Maybe in a few hundred years, when this world was at peace and there was no longer any war to live in fear of, they'd develop something similar. Especially if there were experienced tacticians like Gilles still kicking around. *Come to think of it, does Tsukasa like video games?* He didn't look like the sort of person who would be caught dead even watching anime, let alone playing video games, but you could never judge a book by its cover. I'd have to remember to ask him later.

"Well, I'd say your theory is probably correct," Gilles ultimately said as we got up and started gathering our scattered things. "This is absolutely treant country we're walking through. I have no doubt they're attacking the other groups as well. One of the nasty things about treants is that they can perceive an enemy's overall strength. They can't anticipate our idiosyncrasies and combat techniques, mind you, but that is still the main reason they're so hard to take down. Can you guess why that is?"

"...It's probably their main defense mechanism. If I were a treant, I'd use that ability to assess the relative threat level of my enemies and then gather up enough of my treant buddies to make sure we could overwhelm them through sheer numbers."

We were now running at full speed through the woods, but I could see Gilles, his gaze aimed determinedly straight ahead all the while. "We split our party of eight into three groups, and while this is merely speculation on my part, something tells me they didn't send their strongest forces to fight our group."

Just then, a pillar of light shot up from the forest in the direction we were heading. A moment later, a delayed clap of thunder rustled through the trees.

"Yes, something tells me they sent their main forces to attack the hero's group," Gilles continued, his face turning deathly pale as he picked up the pace.

"That was one of Tsukasa's skills, wasn't it?" I asked.

"I believe so. But my main concern is that if we're not careful, all this fighting is going to awaken the Lord of the Forest."

According to Gilles, one of the previous summoned heroes had awoken the Lord of the Forest by accident and had a hell of a time getting out of that mess. And if the previous hero's party had trouble with it, there was no way our little group could *ever* stand a chance. The Lord of the Forest was a great dragon that had been slumbering in the forest for centuries, even back during the days of the great war between Morrigan's four races, and it was closer to a deity than a monster. I understood why Gilles had gone so pale in the face. Humans generally didn't fare well when they faced off against gods.

"Uh-oh. Looks like we've got stragglers!"

As we were sprinting toward the pillar of light, we encountered another group of treants, almost invisible as they hid among the regular trees.

"They were probably separated from the others," Gilles surmised as he looked at them.

In that case, maybe I could test out that idea I came up with earlier. "Hey, Gilles? Do you mind if I take these ones out?"

Gilles agreed, on the condition that he could stand close behind me in case things turned dicey. I stepped toward the treants as Gilles watched closely.

"Welp, uh, here goes nothing! Rocket Punch!"

I cast a swirl of wind magic around my clenched fist, then thrust it out in front of me. Similar to the technique I'd seen Commander Saran use in the Great Labyrinth of Kantinen, the magic shot out in a straight line from me, blasting away any and all treants unfortunate enough to be standing in its way. They weren't vaporized as they had been by the commander's spell, but they were blasted to pieces. It certainly got the job done, but I wouldn't want to use it on any humanoid monsters that would explode in a gory mess of blood and guts.

"Nanase, what in the world was *that*? What did you call it? A 'rock-hit punch'...?" Gilles asked, looking at my hand curiously.

I had heard from the knight who instructed me back at the castle that Commander Saran was an eccentric with an insatiable thirst for knowledge, and something told me Gilles wasn't any different. He was the type that would stop at nothing to learn something once it caught his interest.

My Rocket Punch (patent pending) wasn't anything too complex, really—just a technique where I cast wind magic around my fist and then unleashed it. It was partially inspired by something I'd seen in a ninja manga once—an attack that sent millions of microscopic wind blades flying toward the target, which would cut the victim on the cellular level. The manga had run for over twenty years before finishing, so my memory of the plot was pretty vague, but I was glad I'd remembered not to actually hit the target with my fist, as that could lead to nerve damage. I also remembered a part where the protagonist turned into a shuriken and threw himself at the enemy, and even shedding a single tear when the story concluded, as it had started as a serialization around the time I was born.

I explained the inspiration of Rocket Punch (patent pending) to Gilles as we ran. If there was ever a chance to bring Gilles back to our world, I would have loved making him read the series.

"We're almost there. Prepare yourself!"

It wasn't long before three people I recognized came into view, and my nostrils were assailed by the scent of something burning.

POV: TSUDA TOMOYA

I AWOKE A FEW MINUTES AFTER Satou tagged me out to tremors shaking the earth. My eyes were immediately drawn to the fighting taking place right in front of me. My muscles were so sore from the previous battle that they screamed in pain every time I tried to move, but since I wouldn't be doing much fighting this time, it didn't matter.

"Holy Sword Technique: Celestial Judgment!"

As Satou raised his sword overhead, a pillar of light shot forth from it and singed my retinas. I could feel the immense power condensed within that pillar of light.

We'd all leveled up quite a bit since leaving the castle, both through real combat and training. But even so, none of us came close to Satou. It made sense for the hero to be a cut above the rest, but it felt like for every step forward the rest of us took, Satou took ten or even twenty. Sure, he did get knocked out earlier, but he was protecting me and Ueno. It was clear to everyone that he learned and grew far more from each battle than the rest of us, which was why I'd decided to place all our bets on getting him healed while I held off the treants.

"*Graaaaagh!*"

All monsters standing in the path of the beam were vaporized instantly. This holy sword technique did no actual cutting—only vaporizing. When I looked at Satou, he reminded me of Commander Saran after fighting valiantly to clear an escape route for us down in the labyrinth, and while Asahina was who I aspired to be more than anything, I wouldn't blame anyone in the world for idolizing this Satou.

"Heeey!"

After Satou's technique had annihilated the monsters, a brief silence fell over the forest, before being broken by what was unmistakably Nanase's reassuring voice. I knew that with Gilles on his team, there was little chance of them being felled by the forest's monsters, but you could never rule out the worst-case scenario. Nanase was one of the few people in our class who got along with everyone and would go out of his way to come talk to me in the corner sometimes, so the thought of him dying saddened me greatly.

"Nanase, Gilles! Y'all hangin' in there?" Ueno piped up.

CHANGES

At first glance, neither of them seemed to be injured, which came as another relief, but just when Satou was about to open his mouth to ask what they'd experienced, a flustered Nanase cut him off: "Don't worry about us, we're fine! We need to get out of here!"

As Gilles picked up Ueno (who still couldn't move her legs), Nanase and Satou both lent me their shoulders so we could hurry onward. I could only imagine what the rush was.

"According to Gilles, there's a high likelihood that last attack of yours could have disturbed the Lord of the Forest of Demise, Tsukasa—a monster that even a previous hero's party wanted nothing to do with! We'd better get out of here while we still can," Nanase explained as we ran, and my jaw dropped.

I turned to my side to see that Satou was making much the same expression.

"Lord of the Forest?! You sure he ain't just pullin' your leg?" asked Ueno dubiously.

"Yes, which is why we need to hurry!"

Sure enough, once we'd made it about a hundred meters away, the earth began to tremble beneath our feet, and we all fell over.

"An earthquake?"

"No, a bellowing roar. From the Lord of the Forest he just told you about," Gilles said, his voice a hushed whisper. "It doesn't sound like he's fully awake quite yet, but even so..."

Before we left, Crow had warned Gilles that there was a fearsome dragon in these woods that spent much of its time in a deep slumber. However, if anyone were disturb its rest, it would ensure they were never heard from again. It was hard to say how much of the story was just an old wives' tale and how much of it was true, but I couldn't imagine Crow making something like that up just to spook us.

"...Well, I think it's safe to say we didn't wake him up this time. I should have warned you all about him before we got here though. That was my mistake," said Gilles, walking a few steps forward. He stopped, set Ueno down on a nearby rock, and began crudely dressing her leg wounds. The wounds weren't too serious, but they would make it difficult for her to walk.

"Well, for now, we should make regrouping with Asahina's team our first priority. We'll need Hosoyama to heal Ueno's legs," said Satou, though how we were going to find them remained a mystery. This was a vast, deep wood, and we'd already run around so much that I'd completely lost my bearings, and the only land-marks in any direction were trees.

"Hey, y'all! Look at this!" Ueno shouted from her rock perch as the rest of us mulled over our options. She was pointing at a specific tree up ahead.

"Hey! Could that be...?"

"Asahina, Waki, Hosoyama! Glad to see you're all safe and sound."

When all eight of us were finally reunited, we found ourselves, surprisingly, back at the same small clearing we had originally started from. When we'd arrived, Asahina's team was already there, waiting for us with a huge haul of various fruit. None of them were injured, aside from maybe a few small scrapes. We all laid out our respective findings and divided them equally among ourselves. Apparently, Hosoyama was able to distinguish the edible things from the inedible, so she served as our poison tester. My and Gilles's teams had been attacked by enemies fairly early on, so our hauls weren't nearly as impressive as Asahina's team's. Still, I'd enjoyed catching fish from the river with my bare hands, difficult as it was.

After we all proceeded to dig in, Asahina was the first to speak. "I'm impressed you were all able to make it back here. You didn't use any sort of waypoint marking system, did you? We thought about using smoke signals to guide you back here but worried it might only draw out more monsters. We were starting to think the three of us might have to camp out here alone tonight." Asahina was clearly pleased to see everyone again, as he was being a fair bit more talkative than usual.

Hey, these fish taste just like sea bream, even though they look a lot more like carp. Pretty tasty! We'd simply grilled the fish and seasoned them with what little salt we had left, so it was a fairly primitive dish, but as people always said, an empty stomach was the greatest seasoning of all. I listened in on my teammates' conversations as I stuffed my face with bite after bite.

Whenever it came time to determine our next course of action, it was usually Asahina or Satou who made the big decisions. Occasionally Gilles would throw his hat in the ring and offer alternate suggestions, but he generally kept pretty quiet and went along with what we decided. After hearing Asahina talk so much, despite almost never opening his mouth in the classroom,

I began to wish I could hold conversations with him too someday. His manner of speaking reminded me a bit of Oda's, though he probably didn't realize it. I wondered if one of them was trying to emulate the other, or if their speech patterns had simply rubbed off on one another.

"We actually have your waymarkers to thank for that, Asahina," said Satou with a sheepish smile in response to Asahina's query as to how we found our way back.

Everyone had seen that Asahina was leaving marks on the trees, but our team figured that because we were only going to be heading one direction, there wasn't really a need to mark our path. Therefore, any unnatural carvings in the trees meant that Asahina's group had passed through that area, so it stood to reason that as long as we followed only the marks on real trees and not those on monsters, we would eventually find our way to his team. And luckily for us, Ueno had spotted one such waymarker right after Gilles finished dressing her wounds.

After Satou finished thanking Asahina for his efforts, he turned to face the rest of us with a solemn look on his face. "It also sounds like I got hit with another curse somehow, which put all of you in danger. For that, I'm really sorry," he said, bowing his head extremely low.

I gained a newfound respect for him at that, especially since he could have kept quiet about the curse and no one would have known. The curse was already broken, so it wasn't a threat to us anymore, and neither I nor Ueno had the intention of revealing that detail to the others.

"I see. So you were already under that curse when you suggested we split up." Asahina had thought Satou put us in groups with people we didn't mesh well with in order to bolster our overall teamwork, but even given Satou's style of leadership, I found it hard to imagine he would try such an untested method in such a dangerous place where one small slip-up could mean death.

"Correct. If it hadn't been for Tsuda's quick wits and Ueno's help, or Gilles and Nanase telling us about the Lord of the Forest, we probably never would have made it back here," Satou replied, head still lowered in shame.

The rest of us looked at each other.

After making eye contact for a while, Hosoyama took the initiative and responded on behalf of us all. "Raise your head, Satou. As our leader, you may have a heavy burden to bear when it comes to making decisions like this, but that doesn't mean we expect you to shoulder it alone," she began. Obviously, hindsight was twenty-twenty, but the important thing was that none of us had died, and we were still united in our goal of making it home. "The only mistakes you made today were not taking more aggressive measures to avoid being cursed, and trying to bear all of the team's burdens alone. We may be getting closer to the demon continent, but we're still firmly in beastfolk territory. If we can't even handle this much as a team, then there's no way we'll stand a chance against the Demon Lord, let alone at making it back home. We all need to work on improving ourselves, not just *you*."

Hosoyama looked around at the rest of us for agreement, and we all nodded our heads. Satou bit his lip and raised his head with a relieved expression, as though a large weight had been lifted off his shoulders. She was right, though—if we couldn't handle the monsters here, we'd be toast against the monsters up ahead. Personally, I felt like I'd gained a lot more determination during my battles, but it still wouldn't be enough. I needed to hone my skills and temper my mind a lot more.

I needed to be strong enough to fight alongside Asahina.

"Well, now that our bellies are full and our minds are at ease, I'd say it's about time we discussed our next move," said Gilles.

I looked up as Gilles laid a large map in the center of our circle so everyone could see. It wasn't anything like the highly detailed atlases we used back in school, but a crudely drawn map. Still, I had a feeling that ancient maps of Japan would have been no more detailed, so it was probably just a testament to how accustomed we'd grown to modern luxuries.

"This is a map I drew from memory based on the one we had back at Retice Castle. I know it's quite primitive, and I apologize for my lack of artistic talent, but I'm afraid it will just have to do," said Gilles, before pointing his finger at the northern half of the leftmost of the four islands on the map. "This is about where we are right now. I've drawn a magnified version of this area, which is right here."

He pulled out another map and laid it on top of the first. This one showed an enhanced view of the forest itself. "At our current pace, we should be able to make it through the forest to the rendezvous point in another thirteen days. But that doesn't take into consideration any time for rest or enemies we might encounter, so perhaps a more realistic estimate would probably be about thirty days."

So it would take an entire month, basically. You could snail mail a package all the way around the world in less time than that back where we came from, but this world had neither trains, planes, or automobiles. We truly were blessed to have been born in the era we lived in.

"And if we aren't there by the time Akira catches up to us, who knows what he might say..." Satou whispered, grimacing. He clearly hadn't intended for the rest of us to hear that, but we all did, so he could only smile awkwardly in response.

I'd only met Satou in high school, so I didn't know that much about him, but even I was observant enough to notice he had a deep-seated grudge against Oda. I mean, virtually any time he did anything, he'd glance over at Oda, only for his face to twist in frustration upon realizing Oda couldn't possibly care less. I didn't understand where his jealousy came from— it wasn't as though Oda was anywhere near as academically successful as Satou, let alone socially. Yet for some reason, he seemed to despise the very sight of him.

Not that I understood Oda's side of their beef any better. As a loner who hid in the back of the class, I'd had even fewer interactions with him than with Satou, but I had certainly observed Oda's obliviousness. It was like he had a different way of looking at the world, and he gave off an aura that suggested he never paid attention to anything that was happening right in front of him— as though his mind was always wandering off somewhere else.

I had no hope of ever truly understanding what made Oda tick, yet after being summoned to this world alongside him and having several close brushes with death, there was one thing I'd learned: for Oda, life had always been a struggle, even before coming here. I wasn't sure if he had a terrible home life, or his family was suffering from enormous debt, or what, but I could tell he'd been living his life under constant pressure. He wasn't anything like the rest of us, passing through each day on inertia alone—for him, every day was an uphill battle. And that hadn't changed one bit after coming here, either—he still had a single-minded focus on living to see the next day and making it home safely.

I couldn't help but wonder if that was what Satou found so annoying about him. Because no matter what we did, we could never get Oda to spare a single thought for the rest of us. He simply sat alone, his mind focused on whatever it was he needed to do to move forward. Personally, I didn't mind it all that much, but it seemed like Oda's behavior didn't sit well at all with Satou. His frustration had reached a boiling point now that Oda had spent all his time with his new companions, like Amelia and Night, despite the fact we had all known him longer and shared the same goal as him. Though it seemed Satou recognized Oda had little choice but to leave us in Retice when he did, especially since we were all still under the effects of a curse.

One thing was for sure though: they both had their own personality issues, and I didn't envy Asahina one bit for having to be the mediator between the two.

POV: ODA AKIRA

I T WAS A DIM NIGHT, barely lit by the light of the moon—long after most of the city had already gone to sleep. I'd come to a part of the city not far from the estate where I'd killed Gram mere days before. Our group had already made its way out of the city, but then I remembered a bit of unfinished business I needed to take care of. Crow, Lia, and Amelia were camped out on the outskirts of town, waiting for me to finish what I came here to do. Night was, as always, perched up on my shoulders.

"This must be the place..."

I came to a stop at a place near Gram's residence which, despite being in the middle of the city, was not a place many citizens took notice of for it was concealed by a unique barrier and thus appeared to the naked eye as nothing more than a vacant lot. The barrier posed no obstacle for someone with World Eyes like myself.

If I were ever in a position where I needed to keep someone hidden from the outside world, I figured I'd try to hide them underground. As long as you hid the entrance well enough, most people would be totally oblivious to the fact that there were underground chambers just beneath their feet. It struck me as ever so slightly humorous that Gram and I seemed to have similar thought processes when it came to such matters. But the labyrinthine layout of the city of Uruk made it the ideal sort of place for one to hide just about anything.

"Shadow Magic, activate."

At my command, the shadows swallowed the illusory barrier whole, being careful not to damage anything else around it. I still wasn't quite sure where my Shadow Magic came from, but it was highly versatile, so I used it an awful lot. I was sure Commander Saran would be over the moon if he could see me now—after all, it was only after he had passed that I learned to properly control my shadows. There was a sound like shattering glass as the barrier broke, then a door appeared on the ground where previously there had been nothing at all.

"You ready, Night?" I asked.

"Of course, Master. Whenever you are."

I opened the door and peered down into a dark cellar, the moonlight creeping in just enough for me to check my footing by. It was extremely dusty, which told me there probably weren't people going in and out of here on a daily basis, and there was a staircase just beyond the door that seemed to connect to an underground passageway. As this was Gram's handiwork, I had been expecting more trickery than a simple barrier, but it seemed we lucked out. Granted, the barrier had apparently kept the place hidden this long, but it still felt a bit anticlimactic.

Suddenly, I sensed that something was off and realized there wasn't a doorknob on the inner side of the door—presumably to keep whatever was inside from getting out. As I stepped down inside, I slowly groped through the deepening darkness, the echo of my footsteps the only sound. The stairwell was just barely wide enough for a single person to descend, but I was losing light fast. It would have been wise to bring a lantern of some sort.

Obviously, there was a reason I'd come here, one I'd briefly forgotten thanks to Crow being in such a rush to get out of the city, but I'd made a promise back in the elven domain to help save their kidnapped family members. Granted, I did tell them I'd only do it if I just so happened to stumble upon them along the way, but still.

When it came time to carry out Gram's assassination, I did a quick scan of the surrounding area, and it was then that I discovered the hidden door. The aftershock of the actual assassination made me want to get out of there as fast as I could, and I hadn't investigated further. But technically, I had stumbled upon the door along the way, so to not come back and check it out would have meant breaking my promise.

"...Feel bad for those guys. I'm sure the elves would do anything to come save their families themselves, if they only had the power to do so."

I tried to put myself in their shoes. If my mom or my sister, Yui, were to ever get kidnapped, and it was possible for me to try and save them but other factors made that a difficult proposition, I'd probably want to ask for someone else's help too. Now that I had all these powers, I'd just go and save them myself. Since elves lived longer lives than even beastfolk, and had far greater mana to boot, they'd probably had to swallow their pride in order to admit they needed help, and I didn't want to spit on their grief.

"Did you say something, Master?"

"Nah, sorry."

After descending what felt like two stories underground, we finally reached the end of the staircase. Now that my eyes had adjusted to the darkness, I could see a lot more of my surroundings.

Suddenly, a voice with a strange intonation and an obvious regional accent echoed through the hall. "...I kin hear ye walkin' there. Ye gonna ask me t'make that medicine again? I already told ye, I'm done makin' drugs that only hurt folk! Starve me if ye wish. I'd sooner die than be a part o' yer wicked schemes! Now let these innocent folk return ta their homes!!!" The voice was shaking with fear, yet I could feel a strong will coursing through it.

"...Aha. You must be Amaryllis Cluster."

According to the documents Night had pilfered, she was the former pageant winner who was being forced to make the drugs that Gram used to turn his mercenaries into killing machines. Lia's people had been seeking her out for quite a while as well, but I doubt they expected Gram's drug operation to be right under their noses; these things always seemed to be right where you least expected them.

Come to think of it, when we registered for the pageant, they used our adventurer dog tags to confirm our identities, but most forms of ID in this world showed one's class in addition to one's name. It wouldn't surprise me if they had noticed this girl's apothecary class and decided they were going to hold her hostage from the start.

"...Beggin' yer pardon? Sh-show yerself!" said Amaryllis, her voice a lot less confident now that she realized I wasn't one of her usual guards. Happy to oblige, I used a mana stone to light a nearby torch. "...An' jes' who might ye be?"

With the torch alight, the two of us were able to lay eyes upon each other. Amaryllis sat behind thick metal bars, along with several women huddled together on the ground for warmth—and not just beastfolk women, but elves and humans too. It suddenly hit me just how much colder it was down there compared to the surface, and many of the women were shivering, their lips purple. We needed to get them somewhere warm as quickly as possible.

"...We'll talk later," I said. "We need to get you guys out of here."

With a single flourish of my daggers, I cut through the iron bars, yet the women were not so quick to celebrate their freedom. They all turned their eyes to a single girl among them.

"Let us get one thing straight first. Can we trust that you're on our side?" asked the human girl, whose beauty was such that she stood out even among the gorgeous elven ladies around her. Her manner of speaking was much more formal now, and her previous rough accent was gone entirely, yet it was still the girl who'd yelled out antagonistically when we'd first arrived—the one known as Amaryllis Cluster. Apparently, even the elves and beastfolk had acknowledged her as their leader. Or at the very least, they seemed to trust her with their lives.

"I think you could say that, yeah," I responded. "After all, I'm here on orders from Amelia, princess of the elves, and Lia, princess of Uruk. But if you can't trust either of them, feel free to stay down here and rot, I guess."

I was only namedropping Amelia and Lia for effect, but I was fairly sure they wouldn't mind. Even if Lia wasn't actually a princess anymore, the two of them *were* aware of and sympathetic to these prisoners' plight. And it was imperative I got the prisoners out of this dreary, freezing dungeon as quickly as possible, so I could simply apologize for this little white lie later. Just as I expected, the elven and beastfolk women among the group became visibly more at ease upon hearing those two names. Amaryllis, seeing her companions reassured, gave a little nod.

"I apologize for my previous impertinence. If your intent is to truly rescue us, we would be forever grateful," she said, prostrating herself before me with such perfect form that it reminded me of the little worker bee Liam back in the elven domain. It occurred to me Amaryllis was probably from Yamato, based on her gestures and her previous lowborn accent.

"You can be grateful to me all you want, but only after I see you all to safety. All who are able-bodied, help those who can't stand up on their own. If anyone can't walk at all, Night and I will carry you."

Night nodded, then hopped down from my shoulders and embiggened himself. A few of the beastfolk captives shrieked at this, but they were just going to have to deal with it if they wanted to make it out of here alive. The only people behind the iron bars still able to stand and walk on their own were a few of the elves. The beastfolk, Amaryllis, and two other humans would have to climb onto Night's furry back. Even the beastfolk who'd been so reluctant to trust a black cat quickly grew infatuated with his warm fur coat and nodded off. I couldn't help but chuckle.

"...Okay, Amaryllis. You're the last one," I said, reaching down to her after everyone else had climbed aboard.

She shook her head and returned to where she'd been sitting. "No, I shall remain here. I have no right to live on the surface any longer," she declared, a fierce will burning in her eyes. I could only sigh in response. She reminded me of Amelia—stubborn to the point that she'd condemn herself to death. "I spent many moons crafting horrible tinctures for villainous ends simply so that I might live another day. I must atone for my sins... It was the other captives you were sent here to save, no? Please, forget about me and be on your way."

Unfortunately for her, my brain didn't have a convenient Memory Erasure function, nor did I possess Amelia's father's Forgetting skill. I instructed Night to take the other women up to the surface ahead of me, and he nodded before dashing off toward the staircase. Amaryllis seemed relieved by this, but only until I walked over and sat down in front of her. The torchlight illuminated her sickly pale face, which possessed a very refined beauty. Even if she wasn't quite as traditionally attractive as Amelia or Latticenail, it was still difficult to see such beauty reduced to an emaciated husk.

"You've got it all wrong," I said. "I'm not here for the reasons you think I am."

I had only sent the other women up to the surface without

her because they seemed to be fast approaching their physical and mental breaking point, and while I had said they were free to stay down here and rot if they wanted, I had no intention of actually leaving anyone behind. And that included Amaryllis.

"...Whatever do you mean? If you are truly here on behalf of the elven and Uruki princesses as you claim, then I assume that means Gram's crimes have been exposed for the entire world to see, as well as the similarly horrible atrocities my medicines have wrought. Otherwise, you would never have found this place." She looked at me with renewed skepticism in her eyes.

I sighed and prepared to let the cat out of the bag. "Technically, I'm not here on orders from Amelia or Lia. That was just a little white lie I told to make the elves and beastfolk feel more at ease. In reality, I'm only here because of a promise I made."

"Oh? And what promise would that be?" she asked, cocking her head curiously. This girl would not have made a very good poker player, because her emotions were written all over her face. I decided to satiate that curiosity.

"I was asked to save you, and everyone else being held captive, by the men of the elven domain...and apparently I have a hard time saying no to that sort of thing."

Though, I probably would have rescued them even if I hadn't made that promise. The elves hadn't asked me to save the beastfolk women or Amaryllis, after all, but I wanted to do it. The moment I started comparing Amaryllis's sheltered lifestyle to Amelia's back when we'd first met, it was all over for me.

POV: GILLES ASTI

W E ALL WISHED to make our way through the forest as quickly as possible, but it was proving to be a much more arduous trek than we could have imagined, and the frequent monster encounters weren't helping matters.

"It's headed your way, Nanase!"

"Roger that! Get down on the ground, you freak of nature! Wind Blade!"

Heeding Asahina's warning, Nanase let loose his magic spell. It was a starter-level spell that all wind mages learned early in their training, yet when Nanase cast it, it was powerful enough to be on par with intermediate spells. If I looked closely enough, I could even see wind gathering around him. Were we not in the midst of battle, I would have asked how he managed to get so much power out of that spell. It wasn't long before the flying monster we were fighting fell to the ground. Asahina and Satou, seeing their opportunity at last, held their weapons aloft.

To explain how we'd found ourselves stuck in yet another combat scenario, we have to go back in time about five minutes. Having successfully escaped from the treants, reconvened, and eaten our fill, we began walking through the forest, carving a path where there was none before, hoping to avoid as many monster encounters as possible.

"So hey, what was up with those weird balls they gave us for the labyrinth, anyway?" Waki asked, following one of his tamed cats.

A good question. The investigation report following the minotaur ambush on the beginner levels the Great Labyrinth of Kantinen stated that it was the monster-repelling smoke bomb Satou had thrown which had lured the beast. While I was originally quite determined to get to the bottom of the mystery, it wasn't long after that incident that Commander Saran was killed, and everything was thrown off course. It was also then that Akira, the boy who'd been vital in slaying the minotaur, was forced to flee the castle—something I was fairly certain the royal family had planned for all along.

"I don't know," said Satou. "All I know is that the last one I threw was handed to me by the princess herself. We were using them to try to *avoid* any more unnecessary fighting... Though come to think of it, I think the last one I threw was a different color than the rest..."

At this, my eyes widened. You could buy smoke bombs for repelling monsters as well as luring them in at any Adventurer's Guild branch—and their respective functions were denoted by different-colored smoke. This was information we had been planning to teach the heroes, but it seemed the royal family had beaten us to the punch.

"Do you remember what color it was?!" I demanded.

"W-well, not vividly, but I wanna say it was red?" he replied, turning his head to the sky as he racked his memory.

I knew it, I thought to myself, my hatred for the self-serving royal family somehow growing even deeper. "Well, as I'm sure you probably surmised based on its different color, red smoke bombs are actually designed to *lure in* more powerful monsters.

They're normally used by higher-level adventurers for the pur-
poses of leveling up without having to descend all the way to the
deepest levels of the labyrinth. So, the princess gave you smoke
bombs that would not protect you from harm but actually put
you in *grave* danger. Though we knights should have done a better
job of checking your equipment. Forgive me."

I bowed my head low, but Satou quickly ordered me not to in
a fluster. I wished the royal family could have had even a fraction of
his humility. I remembered a time when they hadn't been such awful
humans, content to use their subjects as tools to advance their power.
We knights were supposed to protect the king from his enemies, but
in reality, it was his people who needed protection from him.

"Still, why would they try to sabotage *Satou*, of all people?" I
pondered aloud.

"Who knows? Maybe they decided they didn't need a hero
anymore," said Nanase.

I tilted my head and thought about this a while. Even before
the actual summoning took place, after the queen had passed
away, I could tell that the royal family had developed an obsession
with the hero summoning ritual. The queen's death was when
things started to turn. The king from long ago was a kind and
generous man who always went out of his way to spare a thought
for us knights...and a far cry from the king of now.

"...Well, in any event, we'd better get moving. Let's just pray
we don't run into any more monsters, shall we?" I said, trying to
change the subject.

"Uh, Gilles? Where we come from, that's called 'jinxing it,'" said Nanase with a weary look on his face. For once, I was grateful Akira wasn't around because I knew he wouldn't have let me get away with blatantly avoiding the topic like that.

We walked for a while, until suddenly a great shadow fell over us, and we all drew our weapons immediately. I gripped the hilt of my sword, all the while admiring how these children had grown in the short time they'd been in Morrigan. Hesitantly, I turned my head to look up at the sky, and my words caught in my throat.

"Is that a *whale*?!" cried Satou, apparently recognizing the giant behemoth floating through the sky and blocking the light.

It had an enormous mouth and a body like a fish. When I strained, I could just make out a few sharp fangs, as well as beady black eyes staring down at us. It had apparently decided we were prey, and I felt altogether silly for how soon this had happened after praying for no more enemy encounters.

"If we want to have any hope of doing serious damage to that thing, we'll need to find some way to bring it down to the ground!" I cried. "Try to use long-range magic to knock it out of the sky!"

Right on command, Asahina let loose a spell without even missing a beat. "...O purgatory flames, bring forth thy conflagration and reduce these heretics to ash! Inferno!!!"

Asahina's flames shrouded the sky. Inferno was a high-level fire spell and more than powerful enough to consume the giant beast and incinerate it whole. There were few people in this world who could handle such advanced magic, which only made it all the more impressive to see an outsider with such a strong grasp of it.

"...It didn't work?!"

And yet, when the flames subsided, the monster emerged, completely unscathed. The only noticeable difference was that it was flying a lot closer to the ground than before.

"It could be immune to magic! Try to bring it all the way down!" ordered Satou, and everyone tried out their own ranged attacks.

"It's no use! Nothing's working!" Waki cried out in despair.

It was clear our attacks were landing, even if we couldn't use our full power, but the behemoth didn't even budge. I'd encountered several enemies in my life that were immune to magic, but this creature seemed immune to Waki's arrows, and Hosoyama's and Ueno's poison throwing daggers as well. They all struck the beast, yet it remained flying, unharmed.

I let out a sigh despite the tense situation. *The closer we get to the demon continent, the more even normal monsters will begin to defy expectation.* Now I could see why Akira was so reluctant to let these kids—or myself—tag along. Though he sure had a strange way of showing his concern for their well-being. I had only known him a short while, but he reminded me of a certain socially awkward blacksmith in that regard.

"It's attacking!" yelled Tsuda, holding up his greatshield to protect the rear fighters. He had grown quite a bit since we entered this forest—perhaps that was what such a dangerous place did to a person.

Wait! Now's not the time for thoughts like these! I rebuked myself.

The beast let out a bellowing wail, then fired hundreds of sharp, needlelike objects from its belly. I deflected as many as I could with my sword, then looked around to see if the others were safe. I smiled in relief; though a little worse for wear, the fire in their eyes had not yet been extinguished.

"It's headed your way, Nanase!" I cried.

Suddenly, I felt like I could understand why Crow had taken on Princess Amelia as his pupil, despite saying for years that he was done mentoring others. To see one of your own protégés actively growing and improving was one of the greatest feelings in the world. It made me want to stick around as long as I could, just to see where these kids ended up.

"Roger that! Down to the ground, you freak of nature! Wind Blade!"

POV: TSUDA TOMOYA

OUR ATTACKS WEREN'T WORKING, which meant we were helpless to do anything but defend ourselves. It seemed this forest was intent on testing our mettle through trial after trial.

"Dual Blade Technique: Chaos Edge!"

With nigh-unseeable speed, flashes of white and silver light crossed paths as Asahina drew his blades and attacked the monster which Nanase had brought to the ground, yet even this didn't scratch the beast's hide.

"Graaaaagh!"

Satou swung his sword down with immense fervor, only for it to be deflected as well. Nanase continued casting his wind magic from the rear to keep the whale pinned to the ground, but he couldn't keep doing that forever. Neither magic nor physical attacks seemed to be doing any damage to the monster—it was seemingly invincible.

"Please don't give up!" I cried.

I was standing right in front of the whale, struggling to support my greatshield as I protected Hosoyama, Ueno, and Waki behind me. I couldn't let the monster's needles, with their shimmering and obviously poisonous tips, hit any of our three support members. Slowly, I began taking a few steps back, trying desperately to come up with some sort of plan, when a lone figure dashed out from behind me.

"Hosoyama?!" I gasped.

"What are you doing?!" Ueno cried.

Hosoyama sprinted toward the beast while dodging its attacks with such speed and fluidity that I had to wonder if she'd been secretly taking ninja lessons in her spare time. She seemed to have a goal in mind, yet I couldn't possibly imagine what it was. I knew her well enough to know she wouldn't do something so brash without a plan, though.

Asahina, Satou, and Gilles all looked utterly astonished and immediately tried to move in to protect her. Nanase was too focused on maintaining his magic to notice, but with Gilles at her side, she would probably be fine. However, the look on her face said she was the one with the plan, and, though her voice was too distant for me to make out, she seemed to be quickly laying it out to the others. My two less agile teammates and I were stuck in place, blocking the enemy's needle attacks and creating an opening for the others to attack. Which I didn't mind, given that we probably wouldn't have been able to contribute much offensively, but it would have been nice to at least be given a heads-up. This whole thing was taking years off my life.

"All right, let's do this!"

At Gilles's signal, the three attackers began assaulting the monster simultaneously. They were all attacking the exact same spot on its hide, with a fluidity to their teamwork and attack order that allowed them to never get in each other's way, which was pretty impressive considering they hadn't practiced. Though perhaps the most impressive thing was that Gilles was keeping up, despite not having the initial stat advantage that all of us summoned heroes received.

"Now, Hosoyama!"

It was hard to see from where I was, but it seemed Asahina, Satou, and Gilles had cooperated to bore a hole in the beast's thick hide, though it was only big enough for someone Hosoyama's size to stick her index finger in. Still, this meant the beast was not actually impervious to our attacks—even if it took a hero, a samurai, and a knight all working together to the best of their ability to even put a dent in the thing. It spoke volumes to Hosoyama's observational skills that she was able to notice our attacks were indeed damaging the beast while the rest of us were too busy panicking, thinking that the monster was invincible. I'd heard it said that a woman's true strength only became apparent when her back was against the wall: at least in this case, it seemed completely accurate.

"REEEEEEEEEEEEE!!!"

The beast bellowed in despair, and its attacks weakened before ceasing entirely. I kept my shield up, just to be safe, though I could only assume the attackers had rendered the beast completely incapable of further attacks. Ueno and Waki hesitantly stepped out from behind me, and we all cautiously made our way over to the beast. Asahina, Satou, Gilles, and Nanase, who'd been keeping the beast pinned down the entire time, were all gathered around Hosoyama. Just how in the world had she pulled it off?

"You absorbed its *HP?!*" Waki gaped, his cheeks stuffed full of meat.

We had all gathered around a fire on which we were roasting the slain whale monster's flesh, eating only the edible parts. After it was dead, its hide became soft enough to cut through with an ordinary knife, and it was Hosoyama who suggested we eat it (after using her poison-testing abilities to make sure it was safe, of course). Hesitantly, I asked if she was really sure it was safe for us to eat, to which she replied with a hearty nod, grinning from ear to ear. I didn't know how she could be so certain, but I had to trust her.

I still hadn't grown accustomed to eating the monsters we killed, but there was no denying they were far more delicious than plain old livestock meat. I'd been told it had something to do with the small amount of mana flowing through bodies after death. Every time we went to an Adventurer's Guild branch, the waitresses always heartily recommended monster flesh as the special of the day. Apparently, even retired adventurers couldn't get enough of it.

"Yep. It's pretty much the exact opposite of healing magic, which uses your own mana to restore someone else's HP. I was inspired to teach myself after watching Yuki do her disenchanting. It was pretty tough to perfect, since you can't really 'feel' HP the same way you can feel mana, but I eventually got it down pat. It's called *Guzzler*."

Hosoyama seemed awfully proud of herself as she made a peace sign and smiled from ear to ear, but all I could think was what a *disgusting* name that was the skill. It made her sound like a human garbage disposal that would devour literally anything— even literal trash. First the poison-testing thing, now this... I was beginning to have concerns about the direction in which Hosoyama's life was heading.

"That said, you have to be touching your target for it to work, and it won't work through thick hides like the one on our blubbery friend here, but keep it in mind as an option, okay?" she implored, and I couldn't help but nod.

Satou, however, seemed less than amused. "It's a good thing that strategy worked out this time, but next time we might not be so lucky. And what were you thinking, running out from behind Tsuda's shield like that without even telling him? What if you had startled him and he loosened his grip on his shield? You could've killed him, Ueno, *and* Waki—not to mention yourself—through your own carelessness!"

I was surprised at his unnecessarily harsh tone. I'd never known Satou to get so spun up at anyone but Akira, and seeing him frowning angrily was a sight to behold. He continued raking Hosoyama over the coals, even after she'd hung her head in shame.

"I may be the hero, but I'm not a superhero. I can't protect all of you at once. Next time you feel like trying something like that, you'd better talk it over with your companions first, and get someone else to go with you. I refuse to lose even one of our party members, especially over a stupid mistake."

"...You're right. I'm sorry, that was careless of me."

"It's fine. As long as you realize what you did was wrong. Now eat your food."

An intense fire burned in Satou's eyes as he watched Hosoyama obediently bow her head.

POV: WAKI DAISUKE

IF THERE WAS ONE WORD that perfectly encapsulated the way I felt deep down in my heart right now, it would be "pathetic." Ever since we entered the forest...or really, ever since we ran away from the castle and had our first taste of real combat, my mind had been clouded by feelings of worthlessness. Every other boy knew how to fight for themselves, while I was stuck with the girls behind Tsuda's shield.

Granted, animal trainers like me weren't intended to fight on the front lines, but it was still possible to contribute if you could tame ferocious beasts and monsters. I could only tame small animals currently. I knew I needed to take time and level up in order to contribute more, but I couldn't help feeling restless about how little I was capable of doing. In the time it took me to level up once, the others were leveling up numerous times, which was a normal discrepancy between active combatants and support classes, but even when I tried to train on my own, I couldn't keep up with those gaining experience in combat. And up until now, that was the way I'd always excused it to myself.

"But now this is just starting to get sad, man."

It had been Hosoyama who dealt the fatal blow to that whale monster. Despite being a healer, and having even lower overall stats than me, she still took down the huge beast with a single finger. I'd kept telling myself that it was just the class I'd been dealt that was holding me back, but that clearly wasn't the case. If even a healer like Hosoyama could do more than was expected of her class, then surely, I could do it too. Maybe I couldn't learn that guzzler skill of hers, but there must have been *some* way I could contribute to the battle like that.

"...Guess I'm just too stupid, huh?"

All throughout junior high and high school, I'd treated school as a place I went not to learn but to participate in extracurricular activities. I never really studied outside of doing my homework and right before exams, when all extracurricular activities shut down temporarily. And even then, I still couldn't wrap my brain around subjects that required problem solving and a more creative mind.

"What's the matter, Waki?" asked Tsuda, who'd heard me muttering to myself. He and I had been assigned to go down to the river and wash the utensils we'd used during our meal, though I'd forgotten he was there. He didn't really stand out from the crowd, so it was often easy to forget he was even in class (though Oda was far worse in that regard). I couldn't remember speaking a single word to him, though the way he'd tilt his head and look up at me with that feminine face of his certainly gave me some confusing feelings, which probably contributed to me avoiding him.

"Nothin'. Don't worry about it..." I replied.

"Wait, let me guess. You're still thinking about that skill Hosoyama came up with, aren't you?" he pestered—and hit the nail right on the head. His eyes glittered as though saying "I'm right, aren't I?!" and I had to take a moment to reassess whether this was really the same bashful Tsuda I'd always known. Maybe he'd only shown this side of himself to his close friends.

He seemed surprisingly friendly, so I decided to swallow my pride and open up to him a little bit. I knew he had to at least be smarter than me, so maybe he could offer some advice. "Well, I've just been feeling like if even a *healer* can drain an enemy to death, then surely there must be a way for a guy like me to take down monsters too, y'know? But I'm not exactly the sharpest crayon in the box, so if you have any good ideas, I'd be happy to hear them."

"Hrmmm... A way for an animal trainer to participate in combat..." Tsuda mumbled, folding his arms as he mulled it over. I couldn't help but smile at the sight.

Never in my wildest dreams would I have imagined me, the class clown, going on an adventure with Tsuda, the kid who kept to himself. I was honestly enjoying life in this world a surprising amount. Sure, there were times I got homesick when thinking about my mom's cooking, but it felt really refreshing to not be hassled by everyone around me all the time.

Not to mention, there was no guarantee that time in this world moved at the same rate as it did in ours, so it was possible that that big club meet I'd been working toward was already over by now. It was equally possible this was a Rip Van Winkle scenario, and by the time we made it back to our world, we'd find that hundreds of years had passed. That sounded pretty outlandish, but so did getting summoned to another world. Anything was possible, as far as I was concerned.

"Well, if I had to guess, I'd say animal trainers probably aren't well suited to killing monsters at all," said Tsuda, snapping me out of my thoughts.

"What makes you say that?" I asked, as something bumped into my leg. I looked at my faithful cat companion nuzzling its head against my leg. It was the first animal I'd tamed, back when we were still living at the castle. I scooped up the furry feline and petted it gently on the head. It let out a low, relaxed purr.

"Now, I'm just guessing here, but isn't the whole point of the animal trainer class taming and training monsters and animals?

I feel like you should be thinking less about how you could help kill monsters and more about how you could get them on our side."

I cocked my head. The statement brought us right back to my initial predicament: I simply wasn't a high enough level to tame the kinds of monsters we were encountering. How was I ever going to overcome that fundamental issue?

"I think there's more to being an animal trainer than getting wild beasts to do your bidding. I mean, just look at that cute, widdle kitty! I can tell it trusts you with all its heart, and not because you forced it to, either. Is it really that crazy to think you might be able to do the same with a monster if you approached it in the right way?"

I was finally starting to see where he was coming from. Basically, I had to come up with a spell I could cast on monsters to make them feel the same level of trust toward me that I'd already built up with the cat, something like brainwashing. I couldn't tame a monster the traditional way, but with magic, I just might be able to make it work.

"Magic is a means of making the impossible possible, after all. All you have to do is think and feel it hard enough and the magic will do the rest for you. That's how one of the knights at the castle explained it to me, anyway."

It felt like I finally had hope again, and I laughed. Then I came to the sudden realization that I hadn't laughed once since we entered the forest. I wondered if my companions had noticed and been worried about me. In my one hand, I cradled the sleeping cat, and with my other, I clapped Tsuda on the back (though not as hard as I could, since I knew he was dainty like a flower).

"*Bwagh?!*" he squealed.

"I owe you one, man! Thanks to you, I feel like I've finally got an idea of what I need to do!" I beamed, scooping up the clean utensils and standing up. "Also, you might wanna stop saying things like 'cute, widdle kitty,' just sayin'. Not that it doesn't fit your personality, but unless you actually *want* people to mistake you for a girl, I'd maybe try to work on that."

While I hadn't interacted much with our party members back in the classroom, we'd been living together in this world for quite some time now, so it was hard not to see that they all had their own motivations and goals. Now that I finally had a goal of my own, all I needed to figure out was where to begin. I knew I was aiming for some sort of Brainwashing skill, but I'd never witnessed anything like that firsthand before—which was probably for the best. Still, it would have been nice to have a point of reference, but something told me the curse the princess of Retice had placed on us—the closest thing I'd seen to brainwashing—was a bit different somehow.

After fretting over it for a while, I decided to give up on figuring out for myself and ask someone for guidance. Maybe I could start by asking Hosoyama how she gained a new skill through willpower alone.

"Huh? You wanna know how to teach yourself new skills?"

I approached and asked her point-blank during lunch the next day, when she was inspecting her gear a short distance away from the others. She blinked in surprise at my request. "Yeah," I said. "I know I can't learn your Guzzler skill, but I was talking to

Tsuda last night, and I came up with an idea for an ability that might be a good fit for me, but I don't know where to start when it comes to turning an idea into an actual *skill*, y'know? Is there a trick to it, or what?"

I hadn't used my brain so much since the last time I tried to memorize an entire textbook thirty minutes before an exam (you can probably guess how well that went).

"Aha. I was wondering why you two were taking so long to wash the dishes." She grinned. "Hrmmm, I dunno if I'd say there's a 'trick,' per se. All I did was take what the knights at the castle told us to heart, really."

I scratched my head. We'd each been taught the fundamentals about stats and our skills from either one of the knights or a professional in our respective classes. This meant that we all received separate instruction and learned different things. I assumed Tsuda didn't know what Hosoyama was referring to either, or he probably would have mentioned it last night.

"Er, do you mind running it by me? I mostly learned how to deepen my bonds with animals and stuff like that."

And my instructor hadn't been the greatest—though I could understand the royal family assigning their best people to the frontline classes like fighters or to healers like Hosoyama rather than to a less useful class like mine. It was a meritocracy through and through—you only mattered as much as your class did. Even similar classes like knights and samurais were treated differently.

The more time that passed since leaving the castle, the more grateful I became that we'd left.

"Oh, really? Guess I better make a point of sharing what I learned with the others too, then," said Hosoyama. Her equal treatment of her peers served as a shining example compared to the people back at the castle. She was competent, patient, and pretty cute, to boot. I couldn't even be jealous of her anymore. We were blessed to have both Satou *and* Hosoyama on our team.

"First and foremost, you need a steady heart and a strong mind in order to teach yourself new skills," she explained. "Apparently, this is the thing that trips most people up, especially since it's not something you can measure. Heck, we barely know how our minds work back in *our* world, even with all our scientific advances. But according to the knight who instructed me, one's stats are deeply interlinked with their heart and mind, and there are people who have jobs dedicated to studying the relationship between them."

I felt like I remembered Tsuda saying something similar last night. "So what you're telling me is, I just need to want it badly enough, and eventually I'll figure it out?" I asked.

"No, I think it's a lot more instantaneous than that, usually. That's how it was for me, at least," she replied. This only puzzled me more, but she showed no indication of elaborating further and quickly held up two fingers to delineate the next step. "Okay, moving on. The second deciding factor is mana. As in, do you have enough mana to actually pull off what you're trying to do? If you try to use magic that costs more than your personal supply of mana can handle, you'll be lucky to even survive the side effects of the mana exhaustion. Worst case, the sudden release of all your body's internal mana could cause it to break down on the molecular level. I knew my Guzzler skill wouldn't require that much mana, so it wasn't really a concern for me, but if the skill you're envisioning would cost more mana than your max capacity, you'd leave me no choice but to stop you from attempting it."

I gulped. Her expression was deadly serious. This was the first time I'd ever had a one-on-one conversation with Hosoyama, so I'd never peered deep into her eyes before. They were like whirlpools in that they sucked you in, and I could only nod absentmindedly in response.

"You heard what Satou said to me yesterday, right?" she went on. "About how we can't afford to lose even a single member of our party? Well, I feel the exact same way. I admit, I didn't really feel like much of a member of the team until yesterday, but that's not the case anymore. I need you to promise me you won't do anything reckless either, Waki."

I nodded, understanding that her recklessness in testing our food and running toward the monster had been because she thought of herself as expendable.

Happy to see I agreed, Hosoyama smiled and then held up three fingers. "Finally, it has to be a skill that already exists. The only people who can create entirely new skills are a select few who've been chosen by the divine, apparently."

The first sentence came as a crushing blow, since I was desperate for a discernible goal, but the second sentence piqued my curiosity. "Chosen by the divine? The hell? You sure they weren't just trying to sell you on some cult religion?" I asked.

She frowned and shook her head. "Not at all. There's only one real religion in this world, and it's all based around Eiter, the God of Creation. It's monotheistic, and the vast majority of people truly believe he exists. They don't pray or make offerings to him, mind you, but there are an awful lot of believers, so I suggest you watch your tongue—especially when there are elves around."

Apparently, there was a deep connection between Eiter and elven culture: they were his most steadfast believers. And because elves had such long life spans, and very credible records, there were many folk legends about him that were passed down, making him an even more tangible deity. In contrast, the demons had records that were considered utterly worthless, and many thought this was a result of some sort of cultural reset after the northern half of their continent was blown to smithereens, or that the Demon Lord was manipulating the information his people had access to. I wondered if Amelia believed in Eiter too.

"But enough about that. Let's get back on topic. As I was saying, you don't have to know whether the skill you're trying to learn actually exists or not, because if it doesn't, the process just won't work. What you need to worry about is the amount of mana it'll cost and having a strong mind. But don't expect it to be simple, either. If it were that easy to teach yourself new skills overnight, everyone in this world would be overpowered, and we'd probably have already made it back to Japan by now. If you hit any roadblocks, I'll be happy to offer any advice I can, but for now, just do your best."

And then, with a cute little wink, she gathered up her equipment and headed back to join the others. I felt suddenly warm at the sight and had to fan my face with both hands.

"Damn. First time I've seen a girl actually pull off the cutesy wink thing. No wonder Satou's got the hots for her..."

I couldn't help but notice that he'd been staring daggers at me the entire time I was talking to Hosoyama. And he sure seemed concerned about her risking her life yesterday, while obviously not caring nearly as much about the fact that *I'd* been in danger too. It was the sort of thing I probably never would've noticed back in Japan, but the new me could at least pick up on hints.

"Guessing she'd be the one wearing the pants in *that* hypothetical relationship," I thought aloud, then let out a deep sigh more becoming of a weary old man than a spry youngster like myself as I feared for my classmate's future.

POV: ODA AKIRA

P EOPLE OFTEN used the phrase "untrodden path," but I'd never known what one actually looked like until now. The demons had refused to sustain friendly relations with the other races for several hundred years, meaning the part of the beastfolk continent closest to demon territory was overgrown with dense forests and there were genuinely no roads. We hadn't even entered the forest proper yet, and we had already lost the trail; the fact that there weren't even animal tracks to be found here was a bit unsettling.

Crow was serving as the leader of the group since he knew where we were going and was apparently taking us on the shortest possible route to the rendezvous point. The forest was eerily quiet, and while we occasionally came across spots where giant monsters had rampaged through, there were no other signs of animal life whatsoever. It was no wonder people and small animals steered clear, especially with all the annoying bugs buzzing around our faces.

And, as was probably to be expected given where we were headed, the closer we got to the demon continent, the more monsters we began to encounter. Lia kept barriers cast on us at all times so we didn't have to be quite as cautious as we normally would. Even so, we had to stay on our guard, which certainly took a mental toll over time. Unlike the narrow corridors of a labyrinth, here, enemies could come at us from any angle, and it was exhausting to have to constantly watch your back. I could only imagine how tough it had been for the hero's party before us.

I hoped they'd made it through all right. I assumed they'd taken a different route, though, since there weren't any human tracks. All we'd seen were claw marks and monster tracks of different sizes.

As I surveyed the surrounding landscape, a thought suddenly occurred to me. I had no idea what Gilles was actually capable of, given that Commander Saran had trained me mostly in private. I knew he was at least agile enough to have pulled off that superhuman stunt where he ran along the walls of the labyrinth, and that he was able to do some pretty impressive team attacks, but I wondered how well he could handle himself with only his own sword to protect him. I knew he had Crow's seal of approval, so I'd trusted him to serve as the heroes' chaperone, but would Gilles be enough? Hell, even setting aside whether or not my classmates could hold their own in combat, there was also the very real possibility that they'd gotten lost.

Never in my life had I missed the convenience of cell phones more than I did right *now*.

"Um, Lord Akira? Could I have a word with you...?" Lia asked at one point as we were hurrying to the rendezvous point.

I slowed down to speak with her. Our current walking train had Crow in the front, followed by Amelia, Amaryllis, and Lia, with me at the rear, so we had plenty of distance between us and the others and it was easy to keep our conversation private.

I was surprised at how well Amaryllis was keeping up with the rest of us. I assumed she'd be pretty out of shape after being locked up for so long, but she and the other prisoners had taken care to stay as healthy as they possibly could while stuck in the tiny cell. She'd also served as the group's de facto doctor since, given her apothecary class, she was the closest thing to a physician they had.

Still, she was by no means a combat class, so her stamina was lower than even Lia's. Whenever she started to slow down, either Lia or Amelia would carry her for a while. Seeing the two of them fight over her (usually by asking whether she'd rather be carried by an elven princess or an ex-beastfolk princess) in contrast to her innocent gratitude was a sight I thought I'd never tire of.

After rescuing her from that freezing dungeon, but before meeting back up with Amelia and the others, I made a point to ask Amaryllis whether or not she'd like to come with us. If it were up to Amaryllis, she would have stayed down in that dungeon and starved to death, but my conscience wouldn't allow her to do that. I wanted to save all of the prisoners—Amaryllis included.

She'd claimed she needed to atone for having made the medicines that turned Gram's men into zombified mercenaries, so I presented her with a choice: she could either admit her crimes to the world and live in shame, die with dignity, or come with us and help develop a remedy that would reverse the effects of her concoctions. She'd thought it over before answering definitively with the same fierce glimmer in her eyes I'd seen when she was de`termined to die in that cell: she would make the remedy, no matter what it took.

Lia hadn't said a word to me since I told her a little bit about Amaryllis as we were leaving Uruk, but I assumed she was just trying to put her thoughts in order before having a conversation. Both Crow and Amelia looked back when she called out to me but quickly turned around and kept walking to give us some privacy, having inferred from Lia's expression that this wasn't the sort of conversation they should be eavesdropping on. I honestly hadn't known Crow was capable of picking up on social cues—if only he could be so considerate all the time.

"So, what's up?" I asked once the others were too far away to hear us.

Lia looked down. Then, clutching her hands tightly in front of her chest, she looked back up at me with newfound resolve. "Okay, I know this is probably going to sound really strange, but there's something I feel like I need to say to you, as a member of the beastfolk race," she said.

I gulped. Pulling a "we need to talk" at this specific point in time could only mean one thing: it was about Gram. We'd been too busy for her to broach the subject this morning, so I was about 90 percent positive this was about the man I had killed... My heart pounded. I was terrified of what she would say.

"Hey, we got company!" Crow yelled just as Lia was opening her mouth to speak.

I drew my weapon and went into my combat-ready pose (a reflex I'd developed during my time down in the labyrinth), but Amelia made short work of the monsters with her *Gravity Magic* before I even reached them; evidently she and Crow really wanted to give Lia and myself a chance to talk.

I raised one hand to say thanks, and Amelia gave a quick smile before turning and continuing to walk alongside Crow. The two of them had been talking an awful lot since he'd taken her on as his pupil. Amaryllis, meanwhile, was too busy wandering around and gleefully checking out the different types of rare herbs in the forest to pay much attention to us. I figured she'd be fine as long as Crow kept an eye on her.

"Lord Akira? If I may?"

The little interruption hadn't deterred Lia. *Great*. I really hated talking about heavy subjects face-to-face. "R-right, sorry. Go ahead, I'm all ears."

"Then without further ado: Lord Akira Oda, as a former princess of Uruk, I wish to apologize on behalf of my race for the many troubles we have caused you, not to mention the other races of the world. For committing the unspeakable crimes of human trafficking and imprisonment, as well as the royal family's role in covering it up, and for the way in which I spoke about your hero companions, despite their efforts to save us when the monsters broke free from the labyrinth. I could go on, but it would likely take all day. You have my sincerest apologies for all of the ways in which we beastfolk have wronged you and your people."

I wasn't quite sure what the proper way to react to a formal apology like this was, so I simply patted her bowed head. "C'mon, lift your head up. Trust me, I don't hold any of that stuff against you. None of that is even the worst we've been subjected to since we arrived in this world," I joked. I might have apologized back, but felt I didn't have the right to, considering I did what I did for my benefit alone. "How do you feel about how this all went down? And about Amaryllis, for that matter." When I'd explained to the group that Amaryllis would be joining us, and what our next moves would be, Lia didn't visibly react at all.

"I could never forgive my uncle's crimes... Or, rather, my former uncle. Not for the human trafficking, and not for what he did to Lord Crow's sister, nor for what he did to Amaryllis. I think he absolutely did deserve to die, and probably a lot sooner than he did. And yet..." She faltered, looking down at the ground. "And yet, I just can't accept that it was you who got to deliver his punishment and not Crow. I know you had your own reasons for wanting him dead, but now I worry Crow might regret it for the rest of his days. And even if he doesn't, what will his motivation for living be, now that he's finally obtained the one thing he's wanted for decades? Do you think I don't know what people often do when they feel they have nothing left to live for?"

I hadn't thought she was naive, and I'd considered what Crow might do as well. Crow was undoubtedly in a very unstable place, and I could tell that, now that his revenge had been carried out, he was ready to die at any time. After all, he'd been an old man for a very long time already. Once he'd finished his duty of guiding us to the demon continent, it wasn't hard to guess what course of action he might take.

"You're right. I think that's something neither Crow nor I really thought about before, but you also need to understand that Crow's been living with this misery for a long time, so if he's made up his mind, there's nothing you can do to stop him," I said, and tears began to well up in Lia's eyes.

"I know that. Really, I do, but...do you know what he said to me the other day? 'The moment I decided to dedicate my life to avenging my sister, I lost the ability to even think about my own happiness. And now I've roped in an innocent kid to do my dirty work for me. Think it's pretty safe to say I'm going to Hell.' So he has no intention of even trying to live or be happy again after this. He's resigned himself to Hell itself...and that's one thing I just can't bear to see."

Now her tears were pouring down her cheeks and falling down to the ground. But I had no right to dry them for her. *Damn it, Crow. What the hell are you doing?* I sighed and looked up at the sky. A big whale monster was floating gently by, so I went ahead and hit it with a bit of Shadow Magic to bring it to the ground, figuring we could use it for food.

"Well, let's eat before we do anything else. Then you can start thinking about how to express those feelings to Crow. I'll be happy to back you up. And I know Amelia and Night would be too."

I didn't want to commit Amaryllis to helping out, but I was pretty sure she'd assist us however she could.

POV: UENO YUKI

WAS BEING JEALOUS of someone something to be ashamed of? What about harboring a secret loathing against one of your friends? I knew from personal experience just how easy it was for envy to turn to despair, and ultimately to resentment. That's how it had always been for me. No matter where we went, or how old we got, our relationship never changed. I'd known since long before we came to this world that I was inferior to Shiori.

"Wow! Shiori really can do anything, and she's so cute too! How come you're not more like her, Yuki?"

"How can you be Shiori's friend when you can't even do simple stuff like this?"

"Yuki's such a boy's name too. And why do you talk all funny, anyway?"

When we were little, I was constantly being asked such questions, and while I knew most kids probably didn't mean to be

cruel, they still left deep scars on my heart. Shiori and I were practically inseparable back then, and we did everything together. She was the very first friend I made at my new school after my dad was transferred from his job in Kansai. But as I quickly learned, Shiori was the kid in school everyone looked up to and wanted to be, so I was constantly compared to her simply by virtue of always being around her. From junior high onward, I made a point of staying far away from her and not talking to her until I regained my old happy self.

One would think most people understood that just because two people spent a lot of time together didn't mean they'd be good at the same things, but it actually took me a long time to make that realization. Once I did, I was able to make up with Shiori and talk to her again like old times. After all, what did it matter if she was better than me at things I didn't really care about, or if I still had my Kansai accent—*ya got a problem with that, punk*?! Still, my self-acceptance didn't stop the other kids in class from speculating about the beef between us, and soon the rumors took on a life of their own and it felt like no one even wanted to give me the time of day.

No one but *him*.

"God, you're funny as hell, Ueno! I can always count on you to cheer me up."

"Your accent? I mean, who cares? I can still understand what you're saying, so what does it matter, y'know?"

By then, all the other girls were too busy going ga-ga for Tsukasa, but I'd found another boy who told me what I wanted to hear.

"Hey, Waki! Did I jus' see you talkin' to Shiori over there?" I called out, stealthily trying to ensure she wasn't trying to steal my crush from me. I noticed he'd been moping around ever since Shiori had pulled off that crazy stunt of hers yesterday. Which was classic Shiori, by the way.

"Yep! She was just tellin' me what the trick is for learning new skills and stuff. Do you know about all that, Ueno?"

I could feel my smile twitch. Of course I didn't know. I'd hardly developed my abilities at all since we left the castle because how was I supposed to know what things an obscure class like disenchanter was supposed to work on? I'd probably come away from the lessons at the castle knowing the least about my class, aside from maybe Oda, who played hooky the whole time. But even he had private training with Commander Saran, and I bet he snuck into the castle archives to read up on stuff too.

Meanwhile, I didn't know a darn thing. While everyone else was training in their respective fields, I'd spent most of my time cooped up in my room. Even if I wanted to go looking for books related to disenchanting, we heroes were forbidden from entering the castle archives. Commander Saran was working on figuring out a lesson plan for me, but he was so busy training Oda (not to mention his other duties as Knight Commander) that I felt lucky anytime he went out of his way to even come talk to me. Come to think of it, had I ever thanked Commander Saran for his help? My memories of our time back at the castle were pretty foggy—probably a result of the princess's curse.

"Nope, I don't know nothin' about any of that. Heck, I prolly skipped more o' those lessons than I showed up for. Found it purty hard to care about much of anythin' back when we were stuck at the castle, y'know what I mean?"

It was a lie, but it was the best excuse I could come up with on the spur of the moment. Commander Saran had told me he'd call in a specialist in disenchanting for me, but he'd never gotten around to it. And I couldn't bring myself to admit to my crush that I'd spent all of my training time leading up to the commander's death twiddling my thumbs in my room. I just couldn't. Still, I worried that maybe he'd judge me for saying I played hooky while he and the others were training hard. I was practically shaking in my boots, worried he'd think I was a lazy good-for-nothing, but to my surprise, he seemed delighted.

"Wait, so you're tellin' me you broke that curse on Satou and you didn't even need their tutoring to teach you *how*?! That's wild, dude!" he gushed excitedly, and I couldn't help but grin. I was glad to see this world hadn't changed him—he still knew how to tell me exactly what I wanted to hear. Thanks to him, I was able to believe in myself.

"Monsters are approaching our position! Prepare for battle, everyone!" yelled Gilles, and everyone immediately reached for their weapons.

I let out a half-hearted chuckle at how routine this sort of thing had become—that even when we were sitting down to have lunch, we kept our weapons close at hand so we could jump into action at a moment's notice. I wondered if we'd ever be able to return to being our old, carefree selves if we ever made it back to Japan.

"C'mon, Ueno! Let's head back over to where Tsuda's at!"

"Right!"

There was a loud clang as our cooking pot was knocked over. Someone quickly stepped in to stamp out the fire beneath it. *Welp, there goes our lunch. And after we spent all that time cooking it too...* I watched from behind Tsuda's shield as our hard work went to waste in an instant. Monsters would attack us regardless of whether we were on our guard or trying to eat, and we had lost many a meal to them during our time in the forest—so many that I'd lost count. If only we had someone as strong as Oda in our group, we might not waste so much food and end up running away without eating until well past dinnertime, though I realized I had no room to talk, since I couldn't contribute to combat whatsoever.

As someone who'd had the privilege of hiding behind Tsuda's shield until the fighting was over, I resented that I felt useless. And even if Oda were there, we'd just foist all the combat duties onto him, which didn't sit well with me either. *If we're just going to throw one of us to the wolves to save everyone else's skin, then maybe I should just sacrifice myself and end it all...*

"What in the HELL is a *robot* doing out here in the middle of the damn forest?!"

Waki's frantic cry snapped me back to reality. He was standing beside me, cradling his cat and monkey as they trembled with fright, and I completely lost my train of thought. As it turned out, the "monster" that had ruined our lunch was a bipedal robot that looked like a kid's toy from our world but seemed extremely out of place in this one. Though for a robot, its movements were remarkably smooth and natural. Maybe there was a person inside piloting it. Regardless, its silver chassis and the dull light coming from its eyes stuck out like a sore thumb in the forest, and it was obviously man-made.

It was about the size of an average adult and far too solid for our attacks to put a dent in it. On top of that, its attacks came too frequently for even Shiori to dodge (and she'd been able to evade the whale's needles!) and they had a poison effect to boot. It could also switch between close-range and long-range attacks at will depending on how far away it was. In other words, it was basically our worst nightmare; I wanted to know what we'd done to its maker to deserve this punishment.

According to Shiori, it was being powered by mana and probably wouldn't come to a stop until its mana supply ran out. The obvious solution was perhaps to try to exhaust its mana, but something told me that we'd run out of stamina long before that would happen. Oh, and Shiori's Guzzler skill wouldn't work this time, because we couldn't get close to it—even if we could, would a robot even *have* HP for her to drain?

"Hey, Ueno! Sorry to bother you but is there any chance you could cure poison from where you're standing?!" Tsukasa cried out.

Startled, I looked up and saw he'd taken a long-range attack directly to his left arm, which now hung limp. The poison was probably a paralytic. But if Tsukasa were to retreat, the robot would surely destroy Nanase and Gilles.

I nodded and then realized that perhaps there was another reason for the self-deprecating mental tangents I'd been having today. When Waki's voice snapped me out of one earlier, it finally hit me: this was similar to how it had felt when we were all cursed back at the castle. Once, at an Adventurer's Guild branch, I'd heard it was easy to get stuck in cyclical thought patterns when under the effects of a mental interference skill... and suddenly it all made sense. This robot was clearly state-of-the-art—what was stopping it from having a few hidden mental interference skills?

"Hey, y'all! I think this robot's messin' with our heads! Be careful!"

After making sure everyone was warned, I stretched out my arms and tried to move as close as I could to Tsukasa while casting my disenchantments. Thankfully, he was just within range of my detox spell, and his arm began to glow faintly with the spell, though I unfortunately wouldn't be able to reach the others.

"Hey, Tsuda? Can we scootch on up just a bit?" I asked. "I can't reach anyone but Tsukasa from back here... Uh, Tsuda?"

His shield had begun to wobble. Tsuda did, admittedly, come off as pretty dainty—even daintier than me—but this was unprecedented. I looked at his face and, to my horror, discovered lifeless eyes staring back at me. I bit my lip, rebuking myself for not realizing sooner that the robot's curse would have obviously hit Tsuda as well, since he was standing between me and it. Now he was probably thinking about sacrificing himself to save the others like I had been only a minute ago.

I grabbed him by the arm and called his name over and over, but he simply shook me off as though he didn't even recognize me. I was a disenchanter, so I had been able to figure out what was happening to me, but the others probably wouldn't realize until it was too late. How had I not considered this possibility sooner?! However, if I stopped everything to try to lift Tsuda's curse, I wouldn't be able to cure our three fighters if they got poisoned while I was casting. What if they suffered serious injuries as a result? *What am I supposed to do…? Maybe I'm just not good enough after all. I bet Shiori would be able to salvage this situation without even trying.* But as I raked myself over the coals internally, someone came over and clapped me on the back: *Shiori.*

"Hey, keep it together! We'll be in big trouble if you freeze on us now! What are you trying to do? Is there any way we can help? You're the only one here who can dispel its magic, Yuki. We need you!"

When I saw the fierce determination in her eyes, I forgot to breathe. There was a time when I loathed those eyes more than anything else in the world, but right now, they were my biggest source of reassurance. I'd always gone on and on about how much I resented her, but never once did I take the time to examine who she actually was, even when I knew deep down that the perfect goody-two-shoes I was always comparing myself to wasn't the real Shiori at all. I took a deep breath and then slapped both my cheeks at once to get my head back in the game.

"Waki, I'm gonna need you to hold the shield for a sec. Shiori, you run along and help the front line. C'mon, Tsuda, give it here," I said, grabbing Tsuda by the arm. I was being a little rough, but that was the only way I could wrest control from a combat class like him (and despite what I said about him being dainty, he could still easily overpower me if he wanted). Ideally, I wanted to break the curse on him before he tried anything foolish.

"You got it!" said Waki.

"Take care of Tsuda for us!" said Shiori.

As the two of them set about doing as I asked, I started casting a disenchantment on Tsuda. But just then, my thoughts did another 180. It seemed the robot was able to use its mind control magic on us without much effort, as scary as that sounded. And on top of that, it was launching poisonous attack after poisonous attack on our frontline fighters, which left them in an awfully tricky situation. There was so much I needed to do, and so little time, and by the time I finished curing Tsuda, someone else could be under the robot's spell. And on and on and on…

"If only there were some sort of vaccine for this stuff…" I mused.

But then I thought about it some more and was surprised at just how much sense that idea made. Seriously, what *if* we could make some kind of vaccine against mind control? Like a flu shot—how did those work again? I thought I remembered hearing they introduced a tiny amount of the virus into your body so your immune system could build up a resistance to it. As

I'd been hit by its mind control and Tsukasa by its poison, and I'd cured both, I understood them better and maybe had a little immunity to them too. Maybe we could use that to help protect the others. Granted, I wasn't even sure if it was *possible* to build up an immunity to magic, but it was still worth a shot. But then again, what if it didn't work? We were in the midst of a heated battle, and one wrong move could spell death for us all.

Worst-case scenarios ran through my head one after another, until a loud voice shouted down at me from above.

"You got somethin' on your mind, Ueno?!" Waki barked, trying his best to hold up the heavy shield the way he'd seen Tsuda do it.

He'd noticed I wasn't really putting my back into my disenchanting, but when I looked up at Waki, another thought suddenly occurred to me. Hadn't he been saying something earlier about teaching yourself new skills?

"Hey, Waki! What was all that stuff you were sayin' about teachin' yourself new skills? I'm thinkin' I might just be able to do somethin' about that dang poison, if nothin' else."

If I could make the vaccine idea into a skill, then it might just give us the advantage we needed. And if we were lucky, it might even work on the mind control too.

"You serious?! Okay, well, I'll just tell you what Hosoyama told me..."

Time was of the essence, so he had to keep it as brief as possible, but I nodded along with his explanation as best I could. *I see, so for most people it doesn't just happen overnight, and if you're really unlucky, it might end up destroying your body on the molecular level. Got it.*

"You still sure you wanna try it? I mean, if something goes wrong..." Waki warned.

"What, I might pop like a big balloon? Pshaw, I ain't worried 'bout all that."

The light swirling around Tsuda abated as I finished dispelling the curse. After confirming life had returned to his eyes, I stood up straight. Now it was time to find out if I could teach myself a new skill or not. I moved next to Waki and peeked out from behind the shield to tell Shiori (who was healing Tsukasa and the others) that she could fall back.

I closed my eyes and focused. I'd witnessed firsthand the moment Shiori acquired her guzzler skill. One of the perks of being a disenchanter was that I could feel the flow of mana emanating from other people, and I could tell in that moment she was trying to channel her mana into something specific through feel alone.

"Man, this thing's startin' to really get my goat. It can just zoom away and start usin' ranged attacks whenever we get close, and its attacks are poisonous, to boot? *And* it's got some sorta mind control, *and* its heavy metal hiney's too thick for Tsukasa to crack? You'd think someone wanted us dead, but why not just use a more lethal poison and quit foolin' around...?"

I was just thinking aloud now. I'd never been so pissed off by anything in my entire life as I was by the robot. It was said to take a strong will to learn new skills—well, anger was a type of will, wasn't it? I was sure Shiori had learned guzzler by wishing with all her heart that she could save everyone from peril, but I didn't have the heart of a saint like her.

"Seriously, y'all, what's this thing's deal? If it's just tryin' to screw with us, it needs to buzz the heck off! We ain't got time to play with you, ya big heap o' scrap!"

Thinking about how Shiori had done it, I let my mana course through my entire body as though I were about to start a disenchantment, and soon, I could feel the heat emanating from my limbs. Sometimes I'd gain a new skill after defeating an enemy, or raising my class level, but that had never felt like this, which was probably a sign of the different method of learning a skill. Soon, the swirling tempest of mana calmed, and I could feel that something was decidedly different about me—though I couldn't tell you what exactly. Had I successfully acquired the skill? I immediately checked my stat page. When I saw a new skill at the bottom of the list, I couldn't help but do a fist pump.

"Wait, did you actually pull it off?!" gasped Waki beside me.

I ignored him and wasted no time in testing my new skill.

It was called immunization. By design, it was able to lower the effectiveness of certain status effects, including poison, by raising the target's resistance to any ailments I'd either been inflicted with or had experience disenchanting. It wasn't one hundred percent effective all the time, unfortunately, but it would at least work on the robot's mind control, so I was satisfied. Plus, something told me if I got *too* greedy and tried to make a true cure-all skill, my body would end up disintegrating. Teaching yourself new skills really was a dangerous business.

"Hm?"

The bodies of my companions began to faintly glow as I cast it on everyone simultaneously; just because some of us were protected behind shields didn't mean we were safe from the robot's abilities.

"Hey, guys, how d'ya like my new skill?!" I yelled out. "Lowers the effectiveness of poisons I'm familiar with! Works on mental status effects too! But it won't make you completely immune, so still try to be careful, y'all!"

As I finished my simplified explanation of its effects, my party members all cheered. It seemed everyone had been holding back a bit for fear of getting hit with its poison or mind control, but now our three main fighters were able to go on the offensive. Granted, they still needed to find a way for their attacks to put a dent in the robot, but it was still a big step in the right direction.

"Nice one, Ueno!" said Waki.

"Thanks. But it ain't over yet. If that thing's got other poisons up its sleeve, we'll still be up a creek fer sure!" I replied. It was definitely still a dicey situation. All we could do now was hope our frontline fighters could figure out how to kill it.

POV: SATOU TSUKASA

MY WHOLE BODY WAS BATHED in pale light. I had no idea how long this new skill of Ueno's would last, but I knew we needed to defeat this thing before it wore off. I didn't know if I'd simply gotten complacent after a few days without any particularly rough encounters or if my stamina was approaching its limit, but for whatever reason, my sword (which I'd trained with until it felt like an extension of my body) was beginning to feel heavy in my hands. Every time an enemy attack hit me, a searing pain shot through my arms, and my legs cramped up after every move. And now, even my head was beginning to hurt from constantly reanalyzing the situation to ensure I didn't get hit. Needless to say, I was fast approaching my breaking point.

"Damn it... We're so close, too...!"

We were only a short distance away from our destination—the safe house—and we were facing our most powerful enemy yet. The three of us doing most of the actual combat were already running on fumes and only remained standing through sheer willpower. Nanase's magic wasn't effective on the robot, so he was casting support spells on the rest of us instead, but his mana was rapidly depleting. I racked my brain, trying to think of ways we might defeat an enemy that was impervious to all of our attacks.

My first thought was to get in close and try to remove or disable its arms and legs, but it was too hard to even get within sword-striking range, and the material used around its joints was even harder than the rest of its body to protect the weak points; my sword simply bounced right off it.

My second plan of attack was a lot simpler: knock the damn thing over. If we all attacked the same foot to prevent it from moving around so much, we could potentially knock it off balance. When the opportunity finally presented itself and it lifted one leg high in the air, we all struck the other leg, but to no avail—it remained standing. How in the world could this thing be so strong and well balanced? Who the hell designed it? Even cartoon supervillains didn't craft such annoying contraptions.

It was hopeless.

As my thoughts started veering in a negative direction, I lost the will to fight.

"If only I could harness the same power I used back then..." I lamented, thinking back to the fight with the tree monsters, when it was just Tsuda, Ueno, and me. I was down for the count, until Tsuda used one of his potions to revive me, and then I used a holy sword technique to slay all the monsters in one fell swoop. If I could do the same thing right now, we might just be able to defeat the robot.

I hadn't been able to successfully pull off a holy sword technique before or since, which seemed odd since I was supposedly the destined wielder of that very blade. Perhaps the holy sword I'd been given by the King of Retice was a fake. There weren't many surviving records that described what the holy sword was supposed to look like, either. All I knew was it had last been seen in the human country of Yamato before going missing. The only conclusion I could come to was that my successful use of a holy sword technique had been a fluke, and I couldn't count on it happening again.

"Kgh?!"

Just then, I saw Asahina get knocked down out of the corner of my eye. He'd taken a direct hit from his blind spot. With Asahina out of commission, the fragile equilibrium we'd just barely managed to maintain was bound to crumble. Nanase used his wind magic to carry the fallen Asahina back behind Tsuda's shield.

Now our only able fighters were myself and Gilles, with Nanase on support duty. Tsuda didn't seem like he'd regained his senses yet, as Waki was still holding up the shield. This concerned me, because while Waki wasn't exactly a weakling, he didn't have the experience Tsuda had. I was sure that if he managed to block one hit from the robot, he wouldn't be able to block the next. Then there'd be no way to block the robot's long-range attacks.

"Look alive, Tsukasa! It's coming for you!" Nanase screamed, and I quickly snapped back to the battle at hand, only to see the robot had knocked Gilles aside and was headed my way.

This was bad news. Waki and the others were right behind me. Even if I blocked its attack, there was a chance the reverberations from the impact would knock them off their feet. And if I tried to dodge or parry, it might just make them its next target, and that was the last thing I wanted to happen. But what was I supposed to do...?

Unable to decide, I raised my sword and braced myself none-theless. But my legs wouldn't move. The robot was closing in on me fast, and my body was shutting down, ignoring orders from my brain. I was no biology major, so I wasn't exactly sure if that was possible—all I knew was that I couldn't move. I watched my sword hang limp in my hands. I figured this was the end for me. Everything started to feel like it was moving in slow motion. Even if I was to die here, if I could at least find a way to protect the others, then maybe...

"*Yeah? And who's gonna protect* you *then, huh?*"

Akira's words rang through my mind. I couldn't remember when or if he'd said those exact words to me, but the voice was unmistakably his. Though I had lost most of my memories from when I was cursed down in the labyrinth, so maybe he'd said it then. My sword, which still hung limply from my hands, began to twitch.

"*Your job isn't to keep the rest of us safe. It's to defeat the Demon Lord.*"

I could feel my senses returning to my entire body.

"You're right. If I don't defeat the Demon Lord, then who will?"

I couldn't afford to die here.

❚ ENGAGE SKILL: LIMIT BREAK

The still forest air whirled into a tempest centered on me, sending my hair fluttering upward. My body felt alive again, as though my previous fatigue had been a figment of my imagination. With my newfound strength, I easily stopped the robot's attack with my sword in one hand, with no reverberation from the impact.

"But you know what else, Akira? I could never hope to be as cold and heartless as you, either, so I'm gonna protect not only myself, but the others too, and I'll *still* beat the Demon Lord!!!"

Taking my sword in both hands, I mustered my strength. Our brief sword lock ended with the robot being sent flying. Then, my body moving effortlessly and exactly in accordance with each successive thought, I gave chase and drove my blade deep into its metallic hull before it even hit the ground. That same metal which had given us so much trouble was now being cleaved effortlessly in twain, and in a matter of seconds, I'd severed its arms from its body. Another swing of my sword, and the legs were gone too. The now-limbless robot finally crashed to the ground, and the impact blew off its lower half, sending nails and bolts flying in all directions.

"Huff...huff..."

I fell to my knees and gasped for air as my lungs agonizingly burned. I hadn't taken a single breath while I was in my Limit Break state. Hosoyama dashed to my side, not even bothering to check if the robot was truly disarmed. What would she do if it still had another attack up its sleeve? It was too dangerous. But such thoughts died quickly as I struggled to reoxygenate my brain.

"Hang in there, Satou!"

My field of vision went white as Hosoyama cast Heal and Ueno cast Purge on me at the same time. Ueno's other skill had worn off at some point, which was probably part of the reason my body had stopped listening to me—it wasn't just fatigue, but paralysis too.

"That was way too reckless!"

"No kiddin'! I thought my poor heart was gonna burst right outta my chest!"

I couldn't help but roll my eyes and laugh at how the girls' first reaction wasn't to congratulate me but to criticize me for

being too foolhardy. That said, I appreciated having a bit of levity after the battle.

But suddenly Gilles cried out, as if to crack the whip on us for relaxing too soon. "On your guard!! It's not over yet!"

I hopped to my feet, only to discover that the supposedly defeated robot and its scattered parts were vibrating and moving around.

"How in the heck is this thing still moving?!" I said, genuinely astounded. Still, I had the presence of mind to pick my sword up off the ground and use it to guard the two girls as we slowly backed away from the machine. Eventually, the robot's chassis began to levitate in the air, its scattered parts floating back to it. I let out a deep groan. "Are you *kidding* me? It can regenerate itself too?!"

Then, as if in direct answer to my question, all of the robot's parts—even the ones I'd cut clean in half with my sword—began to reattach themselves to the body, until the robot was completely put back together again, good as new. It was almost like watching a video in reverse. The reassembled robot brandished its weapons to attack us once more.

"...H-how the heck are we even supposed to *beat* this thing?" I heard Hosoyama ask in a trembling voice.

Feeling helpless once more, my sword fell to the ground. This time, I really had reached my breaking point. I didn't even have the strength to pick my sword back up, and one wrong move could mean all three of us getting sliced in half. All I could do was glare defiantly at the robot. But just then, a voice rang out from the trees.

"Well, well. No one's managed to give my Rabbot Mk 11 a pounding like that since the Lord of the Forest himself. How very intriguing..."

I looked around, searching for the source of the voice—which sounded much too childlike for a dangerous place like this. And despite sounding like the voice of a ten-year-old girl, it was also rather full of itself.

"What is it? Can't fight anymore? Well, at least you have the decency to still try and protect your women, I suppose, which makes you a better man than that worthless son of mine... Certainly wouldn't say no if a boy like you wanted to buy me a drink."

I looked down to discover a pair of mischievous eyes peering up at me. The little girl was about two heads shorter than me, but it still felt like she was the one looking down on me. Just behind her stood another robot, much like the one we'd been fighting (which had stopped moving the moment the girl appeared). It seemed our savior had arrived. Relieved beyond words, I fell to my knees. My body wouldn't move, but I somehow managed to cling to consciousness. Finally, it was over.

CHAPTER 3

Home Base

POV: ODA AKIRA

"So, what's your plan now, big guy? As far as Lia's concerned, I mean."

Having noticed Crow's sullen demeanor, I called out to him for the first time since entering the forest. He came to an abrupt stop, twigs snapping beneath his feet. Judging from the sun's position, we were moving at a pretty fast clip today. At this rate, we might just make it to the rendezvous point not long after the hero's party.

Based on my information about stats of the various monsters we'd encountered, I'd determined the hero's party would be able to manage on their own (especially with Gilles on their team), but it also wouldn't surprise me to learn they'd lost a member or two along the way. That was less a criticism of their skills and more a testament to just how deadly this forest was. It was little wonder that there were no signs of human or animal life to be found, and I was beginning to worry letting the hero's team travel on their own hadn't been a good idea.

"And why does that have anything to do with you?" asked Crow, eyes piercing through me.

I couldn't help but gulp audibly—a reaction that normally would have elicited a snort or snarky comment from Crow, but went ignored this time as he stared into the forest. Apparently, his mind was in a much darker place than I'd thought.

"Um, Akira? Is something up with Crow?" asked Amelia, striding up alongside me as I stood there, frozen in place by Crow's malice.

I reached out and stroked her face to calm her. "Yeah, seems that way," I responded. "But I don't think it's a good idea to butt in on this one. That's my take, anyway—what do you think?"

Amelia mulled it over and then slammed her fist into her palm as though she'd come to a firm decision. Amelia wasn't one to fret over things for long, no matter what it was. The only time she ever seemed to waffle on a decision was when asked to pick between multiple different meal options, but even then, it didn't take her all that long to make up her mind. But swift decision-making skills were no doubt necessary for a princess like her.

"Yeah, for now, I'll just keep an eye on him too. Though I do think we should probably warn Lia and Amaryllis to steer clear from him for the time being. He's a loose cannon."

I couldn't help but chuckle at that very apt description—it was probably the best way I'd ever heard anyone describe Crow.

"Oi, yew two! Try to keep up, will ye?!" cried Amaryllis from between the trees.

She had been taking a breather only minutes ago but was now apparently raring to go; her distinctive accent reminded me a little bit of the girl with the Kansai accent in the hero's party. Though Amaryllis had switched over to a much more formal and refined register when we first rescued her, she'd fallen back into her preferred manner of speaking after getting to know us a little better. Which was good because, at first, she would only call us by needlessly formal titles: Sir Summoned Hero, Your Royal Elven Highness, Your Ex-Royal Beastfolk Highness, Sir Member of the Previous Hero's Party—you get the idea. She seemed to warm up to people similarly to how a dog would. When we first found her in the cell, she was clearly nervous, given that all her fellow prisoners' lives were potentially on the line, so she went into defense mode until she got to know us better.

Though now that I think about it, that sounds more like a cat than a dog, doesn't it?

"Yes, we'll be right there, sorry! Look, let's just give Lia and Crow some space for now and try not to butt into their business. Does that sound fair?" Amelia asked, and I nodded. Even I didn't want to try speaking to Crow again in his current prickly mood, and while Amaryllis had never known him any other way, I thought it best for everyone to stay away from him right now.

I could tell Lia was relieved after opening up to me a little bit, but the fact that she didn't talk to Crow directly after our conversation told me she was probably waiting for the right opportunity. Her usual lighthearted rapport with him was nowhere to be seen. When we first left Uruk, she seemingly made up her mind and gained a new determination about something or other, but now she just seemed lost—or rather, Crow's ill demeanor had given her cold feet. Ever since we'd entered the forest, they'd both become visibly emotionally unstable, which meant that Amelia and I certainly had our hands full.

"Sounds fair to me," I finally replied.

At the very least, we needed to uncover the true reason behind Crow's foul mood before we tried anything else. Amusingly, the way he was acting right now reminded me a bit of my little sister after being woken up: generally irritable, with even the tiniest of inoffensive things getting on her nerves as a perceived slight. That sort of vibe.

We continued through the forest in silence for quite a while after that. As the monsters we encountered continued to be on par with those in the deepest depths of the labyrinths, I began to feel more and more like the hero's party wouldn't be waiting for us at the rendezvous point. I was of course hoping they'd still be alive, but I knew reality wasn't always so kind. I learned early on with Commander Saran's death that this world could be a very cruel place indeed. And now my ignorance might get even more people killed.

"Monsters, 'hoy!" cried Amaryllis, whose enemy-sensing skills were far above even my own.

Amelia and I raised a hand in response—these monsters might have been deadly to others, but to us, they were small fry. With her Gravity Magic and my Shadow Magic, not to mention the help of a previous hero's party member and a beastfolk princess, our team was hilariously overpowered. Not that we'd ever gotten careless, mind you.

"The heck is that thing? A robot...?"

I watched cautiously as the monster came into view, its eyes aglow. It wore dull gray metal armor that looked awfully unnatural for a monster of the forest, and it soon began taking aim at us.

Yep, that's a robot, all right.

Its movements were smooth and lifelike, yet I could tell immediately that there wasn't a person piloting it. Its joints were all heavily armored, but its body was considerably less so, which told me it was mainly concerned about protecting against attacks meant to hinder its movement. It was clearly a constructed automaton—though by whom and for what purpose, I couldn't say.

Using World Eyes, I could tell the robot had stats, which told me it had been made by a skilled inventor indeed. One couldn't simply give an inanimate object a name and expect it to develop stats on its own. It could swap between close-range and long-range combat at will, and all of its attacks came bundled with a paralytic status effect. And if that weren't enough, it had limited mind control abilities and could regenerate itself at will. Granted, I could probably beat it down over and over until it was too exhausted to regenerate, and Amelia could probably just pin it to the ground using Gravity Magic, but if the other heroes were to encounter this thing, they'd be in deep trouble. Overall, I thought it was a pretty well-designed robot, aside from the childish name, and it could probably repel most of the monsters around these parts without any trouble.

But as we stared at the robot, mouths agape, Crow walked right up to it, completely unfazed.

"Lord Crow?!" cried Lia.

It was the first time she'd used his name since we'd entered the forest, yet Crow didn't react—he simply grabbed the robot's head and, before it even had the chance to attack, crushed it into scrap between his hands. In the face of such rage, Lia couldn't even manage to get off the barrier she was already casting on him.

"I know you're there, you nasty old hag! Show yourself!" Crow yelled with a surprising amount of venom in his voice as the robot attempted to regenerate.

With unbelievable speed, Crow drew a rune of some sort in the air and applied it to the robot, which silenced the contraption for good. Seeing this, Amelia swooned unexpectedly. Even I, who'd seen a little bit of the runic arts when Crow taught her how to use Inversion, knew it was not the kind of skills one could throw out with ease, especially in a state of mind like Crow's.

"Well, well. If it isn't my worthless son. Remind me, how many decades has it been since you last decided to grace your poor, old *mother* with a visit?"

An arrogant yet easygoing voice lilted out from the trees. It had to be the voice of Crow's mother, though she sounded even younger than me—almost bordering on childlike. Perhaps the reason Crow had been in such a sour mood was because he'd sensed her presence. After all, he'd made us switch up the rendezvous point specifically to avoid running into her. Why had I not thought of this earlier?

"You're no mother of mine!" Crow spat back. "Now hurry up and undo the bewitchment you cast on Lia."

"Huh...?" said Lia—apparently this was news to her.

The rest of us all cocked our heads as we tried to discern what exactly Crow was implying. Had Lia been under some sort of trance? If so, then it certainly wasn't showing in her behavior, which was more or less the same as usual.

"Oh, you noticed, did you? Yes, the one I placed on her is a bit different from the others," said a small girl, who came walking out from behind a tree, glaring directly at Crow. Her hair and eyes were the same color as Crow's, though aside from that, the two looked nothing alike. And what's more, she bore no animal characteristics whatsoever—something anyone with beastfolk blood would no doubt have.

"She's human?" muttered Amelia, having checked the girl's stats with World Eyes.

The girl whipped her long pigtails back and forth, amused. "Right you are, young elven princess. Though I would caution you to mind your manners. A less tolerant soul than I would no doubt feel quite uncomfortable being viewed with that ability of yours," the girl said, laying some thinly veiled criticism on Amelia in a way that didn't match her youthful appearance.

Before Amelia could even apologize, Crow lost his patience and threw the robot he'd been clutching at the girl. "Hurry up and break the bewitchment and then get lost, you filthy crone!"

Just when it looked like the crumpled heap of scrap might hit the girl directly in the face, another robot dashed in from behind her and caught the battered husk of its friend. The new robot looked an awful lot like the first one, so I could only assume the girl had created both of them.

"*Hmph*. Very well. As a reward for having bested my masterwork, the Rabbot Mk 11, I'll do as you say." The girl snapped her fingers, and Lia immediately fell to the ground like a ragdoll.

"Lia?!" cried Amelia, who was standing nearby and quickly scooped her up.

"Dinnae worry. She's only sleepin'," Amaryllis quickly determined.

I let out a sigh of relief before turning back to where the girl had been standing, only to find she was already gone, just as Crow had commanded. Something told me this wouldn't be the last we saw of her, and judging by the intense scowl on Crow's face, I wasn't the only one thinking that.

The canopies overhead swayed in the breeze as we made our way through the now peaceful forest, encountering nary a monster. However, while the world around us was quiet, the same couldn't be said of the people in our party.

"Crow, if you keep being all pissed off like this, you're gonna end up getting one of us hurt, so could you knock it off?" I finally demanded. I couldn't allow Crow to keep lashing out at the rest of us just because he had an unpleasant run-in with his mother.

As he shot me a death glare, I realized my words had only awakened the beast within—and all this after I'd decided to leave

him alone until the right moment. I couldn't take back my words, so I just had to roll with it. I psyched myself up and prepared to double down. The three girls, who were all setting up camp, stopped what they were doing to watch the two of us. I waved them off to indicate I had it under control, though I knew full well it probably looked like I had a death wish.

"And don't even get me started on that fight just now," I went on. "What the *hell's* gotten into you?"

I knew what was causing Crow's mood, but I couldn't just leave the question unasked. For someone like Crow to let ordinary monsters take him from behind, forcing Amelia to jump in and rescue him (followed by a stern lecture) was unheard of. And now here he was, trying and failing to start a simple campfire, surrounded by mana stones reduced to mere rocks, the monster lives it had taken to create them wasted. It was beyond wasteful to see so many used on a simple task. To be honest, in his current state, Crow was nothing more than a burden on the rest of us. In spite of everything, it was somewhat of a relief to see a more vulnerable side of him.

I knew I was deliberately pouring more fuel on the fire of Crow's rage, but, perhaps due to his age, he didn't yell. He let his anger simmer down and die off, his expression uncomfortable. Seeing him with a half-embarrassed scowl on his face was certainly a sight to behold, and I couldn't help but see a little bit of my elementary school self in him in that moment. Perhaps even more damning was that his tail, which had been twitching angrily, was hanging limp like that of a chastised dog.

"What exactly were you hoping your mom would say to you, anyway? Did you secretly *want* her to blow her top and go off on you for letting her die right before your eyes?" I felt like I was lecturing a kid.

Crow shook his head, though, and then gasped as if a sudden realization had hit him. "No, it's not that. I just..." Crow began, but then fell silent.

I let out a sigh and then pulled out a tiny mana stone from an inner pocket. "Well, if you say so, I guess. Just be sure to keep up your end of the deal before you do anything stupid, all right?"

I ignited the mana stone and tossed it onto the pile of dry logs in front of Crow. Within seconds, they'd caught fire. It seemed expressing my grievances had paid off, as Crow quickly shifted from an annoyed ball of anger back to his old, condescending self. Amelia was quick to declare that she liked this version of Crow much better, which made me laugh, but then Lia started nodding in agreement. Apparently, this was the first time she'd ever seen Crow lose himself, and it was genuinely bewildering for her.

Meanwhile, Amaryllis, who knew Crow the least, simply cocked her head in confusion as to what we were all going on about and then returned to her concoctions. She'd been making potions every time we took a rest along the trail, though I had no idea what for.

Not long after, we continued on, with Crow silently leading the pack once again. We soon came to a recently abandoned campsite that could only have been made by the hero's party.

"Are they all still alive, do you think?" asked Amelia as she looked at the extinguished fire, obviously concerned for the classmates she'd befriended.

I scanned the area and then thought it over before nodding. "Obviously, I can only make an educated guess, but it looks like some sort of food spilled all over the ground here, and that looks like their sleeping area right over there. I'd say they were attacked by monsters as they were sitting down to eat. Based on the amount of food spilled and the number of sleeping spaces here, I think it's safe to say they were all alive *before* the monsters attacked, at least. Looks like they dropped some belongings along the way, and they didn't cover their tracks either, so we could chase after them if we wanted to."

There was no telling how they might have fared against the monsters, but it appeared they had left behind just about everything aside from their weapons as they fled. We decided to pick up anything that might be of use. *The hero, Kyousuke, Gilles, Hosoyama, Ueno, Waki, Tsuda, Nanase... Yup, they were all here.*

"...Man, they sure managed to forage an awful lot of food from around these parts," I mumbled, looking at the spilled remnants of their meal. The meat must have come from whatever monsters they faced along the trail, but someone in the party obviously had been able to tell poisonous fruit and plants from good ones: I was pretty certain Gilles didn't have those kinds of wilderness survival skills.

"Twasn't a dangerous fruit or herb in the bunch. Must've had someone with Appraisal or Poison Tester or some such skill. Kept all the poisonous ones neat and tidy o'er here," noted Amaryllis as she examined the site, then pointed to a veritable mountain of picked weeds on the other side of the campsite. I couldn't recall any of my classmates having a skill of that nature before, so it had to be something one of them had learned only recently.

"I hope we catch up with them soon..." Lia said wistfully, as she looked down at the scarred ground where some sort of skirmish must have taken place.

As she spoke, I realized that I felt the same way. My breath caught in my throat as I discovered I was much more worried about the hero's party than I ever would have thought. I was even starting to remember their names after years of not caring.

"The monsters get fiercer the closer you get to the demons' domain," said Crow. "Feel free to hold out hope, but expect the worst."

His icy words rang through my ears for a while after that.

"There it is. Right over there," said Crow, after coming to a sudden stop and pointing a short distance away.

Off in the distance, among the trees, was a grand, three-story building that looked only a few decades old. Its outer walls were painted green to blend into the forest, with bits of white here and there that made it look classy. If Crow hadn't pointed it out, I might not have even noticed it. I'd been anticipating the safe house to be an older and more dilapidated building, so I was pleasantly surprised to say the least.

"...Is something the matter, Lord Crow?" asked Lia with concern after Crow remained fixed to the spot, still pointing at the building, for a bit too long.

Upon further inspection, I realized Crow's scowl was not focused on the safe house itself but on the area around it. His expression turned more grim as he scanned the trees and ground nearby. I tried to sense any potential ambushes, but there were no monster presences in the immediate area, so I had no idea what was making Crow so hesitant. The only possibility I could come up with was his mother, but she shouldn't have been living in the safe house. Regardless, I had a bad feeling about this.

"Uh, Crow?" I said, waving a hand in front of his face. He grabbed my hand in a crushing grip and shoved it firmly away. *Well, at least he's mentally all there. Can't have him daydreaming in the middle of a forest inhabited by deadly monsters.*

"...It's nothing. Let's go."

From his tone, it was obvious it was definitely *something*, and if he really wanted us to believe otherwise, he needed to seriously work on his poker face. He'd always been a man of few words, though, and he was starting to fall into old patterns, which was irksome, to say the least.

"What should we do, Akira?" Amelia whispered, having also noticed Crow's odd behavior.

"Not much we can do." I shrugged. "Not like he'd give me a straight answer even if I asked, y'know?"

I followed Crow, who was walking up to the safe house at a brisk pace and without a hint of caution. If he was the sort of guy who opened up to people when they tried to have a discussion with him, maybe he wouldn't have such awkward relationships with his mother and Lia. Instead, his personality held him back from living a truly fulfilling life.

"...Guess we're finally 'ere, eh?" said Amaryllis, her face blank.

We were now close enough to the safe house to see the entire building unobstructed, and the wear and tear was much more noticeable up close. The outer walls were covered in ivy—time had certainly taken its toll on the building, and it looked almost like your typical haunted house.

"Akira?! You guys all made it?!"

Hearing my name, I looked up and saw the hero peering down at me from a second-floor window. A wave of genuine relief washed over me as I raised a hand to greet my classmate. "Yeah. No losses on your end either, I hope?" I asked.

"Well, not exactly, but uh..." He faltered, and my heart dropped. "Anyway, I'll be right down! ...It'll be quicker to just let you see for yourself."

My mind raced over what bad news he might have to share as I waited for him to come down, but when the large doors finally opened, it wasn't the hero who greeted me.

"Hey, guys! Glad to see you made it. You must be exhausted," said Nanase, who checked to make sure we were all accounted for as he welcomed us with a smile.

"Yeah, glad you guys made it too," I replied. "...Er, is something wrong?"

I noticed his face had matured an awful lot since the last time I saw him, as he now looked like a man who'd stared death in the face and lived to tell the tale. However, there were also signs of great weariness and emaciation, as though he might keel over and die at any moment. I assumed it was less that he was starving and more that he was deeply exhausted.

"Well, uh... I think you'd better just see for yourself," said Nanase, echoing the hero's sentiment as he hobbled out and around to the back of the building. Soon, the hero came outside as well, and we all followed Nanase.

"Oh, come now! Is that truly all you worthless fools have got?!"

"Kgh... Graaagh?!"

There was a loud crash, and then the earth quaked beneath my feet. Not long after, someone flew through the air. I recognized the high-pitched taunts—it was the very same voice that had put Crow in such a sour mood.

"What the hell are *you* doing here...?" Crow growled in a low and husky voice.

The little girl, having just sent an armed Kyousuke flying with her bare hands, finally turned to face us as though she'd only just noticed we were there. "Ah, why, hello there, my son," she said. "I was just teaching the current generation of heroes a thing or two. If you'd like, I'd be happy to take this old building off your hands as payment for my educational services."

Her eerie smile, and the fact that she hadn't answered his question, suggested she perhaps didn't realize Crow's animosity toward her. She turned to us. "Oh, where are my manners? I haven't introduced myself yet, have I? My name is Noa, and I'm your friend Crow's dear old mother. Do try to get along with him, won't you?"

With her long pigtails and borderline-gothic Lolita garb, she was indeed the same girl we'd met in the forest who'd bewitched Lia—though she looked far more like Crow's little sister than his *mother*. As we stood there dumbfounded, Nanase and the hero dragged Kyousuke's unconscious body back into the house. From the efficiency of their actions, I could tell they'd already been through this process several times and were beginning to feel pretty worn out. Now I understood why they seemed so relieved to see us.

"Now then. I think that's more than enough introductions. If you wish to enter the land of the demons, you'll need to make it through me first!" said Noa with an evil smirk that matched the classic supervillain line she'd just uttered.

It seemed our personal version of hell was only just beginning.

POV: SATOU TSUKASA

REWIND TO BEFORE Akira's group found our abandoned campsite.

I awoke in an unfamiliar room but tried my best to calmly regain my bearings. I remembered we'd been attacked by a robot as we were getting ready to eat lunch. After a truly arduous battle, I unlocked a new skill called Limit Break, which allowed us to eke out a victory before the robot regenerated and reassembled itself. At that point, we were in deep trouble, until the robot's creator—a little girl—showed up.

Beyond that point, however, I couldn't remember. I assumed I'd fainted from my battle wounds combined with fatigue and hunger, but I had no idea where I'd ended up. It was a clean white bedroom, simply furnished with only the bed I was lying on, a desk, and a chair; there was no sign of anyone actually living in it, at least not recently. Perhaps it was some sort of guest room. After camping outdoors for the last good while, it felt like I hadn't slept in a real bed with four walls and a roof around me in quite some time. The only building I imagined would be in the forest was the safe house, and, perhaps as a result of the relief I felt, or maybe because of my injuries, I fell back into a deep slumber.

"...y...ke up...! Can't you hear me, boy?! Get *up!*"

The next time I opened my eyes, the light of the setting sun was shining warmly into the room. It felt uncannily like twilight back home. Aside from the ear-piercing voice trying to wake me up, of course.

"Hmph. Finally decided to wake up, I see," the girl said, with a holier-than-thou intonation that reminded me a little bit of Akira's black cat familiar.

"...And you are? Where am I, for that matter?" I asked as I tried to kick my mind into gear. Tired or no, there were certainly potential dangers associated with waking up in a strange room with a strange girl in gothic Lolita clothes.

As I reached for the sword lying at my bedside, the girl narrowed her eyes. "Did you already forget who I am? And to think I was kind enough to save your life. Though, for the record, my Rabbot Mk 11 would never have attacked if you hadn't waltzed obliviously through the traps I set along my security perimeter. Some heroes *you* are."

I could only sit there with my mouth agape. The *nerve* of this girl... I'd never met anyone like her in my life. Despite her refusal to answer my question, I *did* finally manage to remember who she was. She was the designer of the irritating robot we'd fought yesterday. I'd been rapidly losing consciousness when she showed up though, so the lapse wasn't surprising. Her striking black hair and eyes reminded me of someone I'd met recently...

In any case, I relaxed a bit upon realizing she was not my enemy. Then, as if to signify my relief, my stomach let out a loud, unabashed growl, and my face turned beet red.

The girl, watching me blush over such a thing, simply sighed. "My, what a vocal gut you have, you slovenly oaf... Well, so be it. One of the main reasons I dragged you here was to get a good meal down your gullet, after all."

I was just about to give her a piece of my mind, but then a bad feeling came over me and I stopped myself short. Something told me it wouldn't serve me well to get on this girl's bad side. I followed her out of the room and saw the rest of the building's interior was just as clean as the bedroom.

"So where are the others?" I asked, fearing for the fates of my companions. I could sense there were some people on the floor below us, but I couldn't tell if they were my classmates or not.

The girl simply snorted. "Well, you're the only one who's been out cold for two days straight, fool. The others are all downstairs preparing food for everyone—something you'll need to help out with starting tomorrow as well."

I didn't know what made her think she had the right to dole out orders, but I decided to trust my gut feeling and not talk back to her, so I only nodded. *Have I really been asleep for two whole days? No wonder I'm starving.*

"Oh, hey! Satou, you're awake!" said Waki as the girl led me downstairs.

"Mornin', Tsukasa!" Ueno said with a smile.

"About time," Asahina sighed.

They all stopped what they were doing to greet me, and my mood brightened. Soon, the others walked in from the next room over.

"Did I hear Tsukasa's up and at 'em?" asked Hosoyama.

"Oh, good morning!" said Tsuda politely.

"'Sup, bud!" said Nanase.

"Good to see you awake. How are you feeling?" Gilles asked.

It looked like everyone was accounted for, thankfully.

"Yes, yes! Enough lollygagging! Get back to *work*!!!" the little girl barked. The fear on my teammates' faces was palpable, and they all scurried off to carry out their assigned tasks like little worker bees. I wondered what she could have done to make them so afraid of her. And who exactly was she, anyhow? Her child-like appearance and crotchety, elderly personality didn't mesh whatsoever.

"Hey, is there anything I can help you with?" I asked Hosoyama as she pulled some tableware down from a shelf, purely because she was the one closest to me.

She shuddered a bit and then shook her head; she seemed uncomfortable. "N-nope, I got this! You just focus on getting some rest, okay? You need it, so try to take it easy, at least for the next day or so."

Well, who was I to tell a healer no? And I was still feeling a little achy, so maybe it would be best to just focus on helping fetch lightweight things and carry them around tonight.

"Now then. I suppose it's about time I explained to you all what you'll be doing next, wouldn't you say?"

As we sat there enjoying our simple dinner of bread, soup, and salad (which, admittedly, felt practically luxurious in the middle of the forest), the little girl clapped her hands together and addressed the group. I felt compelled to ask some questions of my own. *Where the hell did you get these vegetables and this bread? And who the hell are you, anyway?!*

"...Not to be rude, but I think you'd best introduce yourself to these kids before anything else," suggested Gilles, raising his hand. The way he said "these kids" and not "us" told me Gilles already knew who she was.

"Yeah, no kiddin'. We ain't even know what the heck to call ya," grumbled Ueno.

"I know, right?" Waki whispered. "We only came here 'cause that robot dragged Satou off without anyone's consent... Next thing we knew, she was forcing us to do chores and shit and telling us we had to earn our keep."

Interesting. So the others were already well acquainted with the girl's strong-arming. I was honestly impressed that they'd managed to go along with a stranger's orders for two whole days while waiting for me to wake up.

"Ah, right. I suppose I haven't introduced myself yet, have I? You can call me Noa. I'm the mother of your blacksmith friend Crow, as it so happens," she said, and we all froze, shocked by the massive bomb she just dropped. "For as long as you're all here, I intend to work you to the bone, so you best ready for that."

I watched Gilles's face turn deathly pale under her devilish grin.

"To start off, we need to figure out what you each need to work on. Open your stat pages," said Noa shortly after introducing herself. There were plenty of other questions I wanted to ask her about Crow and whatnot, but she silenced them all. She was not taking questions at this time, apparently.

"Display Status!" I chanted for the first time in quite a while, and my stat table appeared in the air before me, visible to me and me alone.

TSUKASA SATOU	
RACE: Human	CLASS: Hero (Lv. 78)
HP: 2150/3200	MP: 4685/5600
ATTACK: 9700	DEFENSE: 8000

SKILLS:

Mathematics (Lv. 7)	Mesmerize (Lv. 8)
Martial Arts (Lv. 7)	Swordsmanship (Lv. 7)
Elemental Magic (Lv. 5)	Intimidate (Lv. 6)
Roar (Lv. 5)	Scout (Lv. 4)
Detect Danger (Lv. 5)	Herculean Strength (Lv. 5)
Adaptation (Lv. 1)	Fleet Feet (Lv. 1)
Harden (Lv. 1)	

EXTRA SKILLS:

Understand Languages	Holy Sword (Lv. 2) Limit Break

When I saw my stats, I was genuinely taken aback. But then I realized I hadn't checked them once since we left the nation of Yamato. So not only were my skills all higher levels, but I'd even learned a few new skills without even realizing it. Some of these were still at Level 1 because I didn't even know I had them, but others like Detect Danger and Scout had already gone up a few levels. Then again, I had noticed I was having an easier time detecting monsters' presences lately—but I thought that was just a sign I was used to combat and travel in this world. Though I wondered why Mesmerize was still my highest level skill, even when I hadn't used it once.

I looked around at my companions, who were all viewing their respective stat pages and seemed equally surprised. They all must have leveled up quite a bit too.

"All done? Then let's head out back," said Noa, pointing to the back door.

I still couldn't shake the feeling that she was keeping things from us, and she sounded like she was about to beat us up. If this were Crow saying all of this, I'd probably want to call the police ASAP... Not to mention, I could tell the others were equally confused by the lack of a proper explanation. I could almost *see* the question marks floating over their heads.

"Wh-what are you going to do with them?" asked Gilles, much to my relief, since it felt like anything us kids said to her would be met with ferocious backlash.

Maybe it was just my imagination, but I'd prefer to let sleeping dogs lie if at all possible. Like mother like son, she and Crow both gave off a foreboding aura that seemed to say "don't even think about it." It made me wonder what we'd done to get on her bad side.

"Why, I'm simply going to make punching bags out of them, that's all," Noa replied. "Because this latest generation of heroes seems pretty frail. If they can't even take a few hits from my Rabbot Mk 11, I don't know how they're going to manage to fulfill their duty."

Punching bags? If she was saying what I thought she was saying, then we might be in grave danger. I could see the corners of Gilles's mouth twitch out of the corner of my eye. Wait a minute—did they have punching bags in this world? Sometimes I had to wonder if the translations I got with my Understand Languages skill were literal or just approximations meant to make things more understandable.

That said, I had a hard time believing this shrimpy little girl was really planning to fight us all herself, so I assumed her intention was to have us spar with her robot. I genuinely wanted to tear that thing limb from limb, but once we got out back, the robot was nowhere to be found. And after we put on all our equipment, it was Noa that curled her index finger tauntingly as if to say, "Try me. I dare you."

"Wait. We're going to be fighting *you*?" I asked without thinking, and she immediately stared daggers back at me. *Crap. I think I just dug my own grave.*

"Yes, that's right. Do you have a problem with that?" she asked sweetly and with a smile. How could anyone look at her and think she was a suitable opponent? Did she even know how to fight?

"Does she really think she stands a chance?" whispered Nanase.

"I mean, even if she does, it feels pretty cowardly for us, with all our weapons, to gang up on a single unarmed little girl, y'know?" Tsuda whispered back.

Overhearing this exchange, Gilles opened his mouth as if to say something, but he was too late. A moment later, the duo of doubters was sent soaring into the air before crashing into a big tree.

"...Huh?" I gaped.

Right where the two of them had been standing was Noa, her fist clenched and thrust high into the sky. The rest of us looked on in confused horror, while Gilles simply gazed up at the sky.

"Sorry, did you think I was just a weak *little* girl? Remember this: in the land of demons, it's the weak who die first! Never judge another solely by appearances," stated Noa with a stern expression. The rest of us, understandably, raised our weapons to defend ourselves. A moment later, I was out cold.

THWACK, CRACK, CRUNCH!!!

After a few sounds I was fairly sure bones weren't supposed to make, I watched as another of my friends went careening into the blue sky. It was like something straight out of an anime. Meanwhile, my thoughts wandered as I tried to ignore the carnage playing out in front of me. *Wow, what nice weather we're having today. Perfect for drying laundry on the clothesline...*

"Come on! Is that all you've got?! *Next!*"

If it had been the overpowered robot sending people flying with single punches, I maybe could have understood it, but instead, it was a tiny girl in gothic Lolita clothes whose true age was yet unknown. And to make matters worse, we were all armed to the teeth with our usual equipment, while she was using only her fists.

"Is that all you've got, you so-called *hero*?!"

She drove her tiny fist into my abdomen, and my feet were swept off the ground. If someone told me *she* was the Demon Lord, I might have even believed them. My back crashed into a faraway tree, and I was knocked out cold for the fifth day in a row.

A few days had passed since then, and I was just awakening from being knocked out again when Akira arrived at the house, to my genuine relief, not just because I was glad to know he and his companions had made it safely through the forest, but because it meant we'd have a few more worthy fighters on our side who might stand a chance against Noa. We hadn't been able to block or dodge a single one of her attacks thus far, but Akira might be able to, and I was itching to have someone put that little girl in her place!

POV: ODA AKIRA

"SERIOUSLY, what the hell have I gotten myself into?" I muttered as I tried my best to dodge the fists flying inches from my face. By all rights, I should have been fast asleep in a nice warm bed, giving my body the time it needed to recover from traipsing through the forest. Instead, I was out behind the safe house, trying to dodge Noa's fists of fury. I wanted to scream: "Can't a guy get a friggin' *break*?!" All these sudden and unexpected developments were really starting to take their toll.

We'd arrived at the house, and then after a quick one-sided introduction, we were under attack by tiny fists. Fists that, despite looking dainty and petite, had just sent Kyousuke soaring through the air; if it wasn't for all my combat experience, I probably would have been right behind him. Thankfully, her punch missed its mark, but the sheer force of the momentum from the follow-through still tore the earth asunder. As I looked down at the gaping hole her fist had drilled into the ground, I grimaced. I wasn't one to talk, but it seemed pretty unbelievable that a mere human could possess such unfathomable strength. Noa, meanwhile, seemed rather impressed with how easily I'd dodged her blow, as her eyes went wide.

"Well, well... You seem to have far more potential than the so-called hero. Color me intrigued," she said, licking her lips with delight.

A chill ran down my spine. I could feel her aura changing: my Detect Danger skill set alarm bells ringing in my head. A gut feeling told me that I should duck (which I did), and within a split second, Noa had whirled around behind me. I felt her fist fly right over my head, taking off a few of my hairs in the process. There was a sound like the wind being torn like paper, and I gulped. Was it just me, or was this girl actually trying to kill me? One hit like that, and I'd be done for.

"Hey, old hag! You tryin' to kill him or what?!" Crow yelled as he dashed over from the sidelines.

"Trying to kill him?" Noa replied, raising her eyebrows. "Oh, son of mine, you do ask some silly questions from time to time. Of *course* I'm trying to kill him!"

I could feel a deep malice beginning to emanate from her tiny body, and I started quivering. Something told me Noa might be far more powerful than even Crow or myself. Perhaps no one here today could stand a chance against her. Behind me, someone gulped audibly.

"If I weren't, we'd just have a repeat of the last generation's hero's sorry display," she went on. "Surely you haven't forgotten? For all your gallivanting and all your training to be the strongest team in the world, the demons still wiped out everyone in your party aside from you and the hero well before you even met the Demon Lord. And you called yourselves *heroes*? Did you forget what you went to the land of demons to do?!"

As Noa continued to berate her son, her focus remained fixed on attacking me. I bent backward, just barely managing to avoid one swipe that nearly grazed my nose.

"That's what I'm here for!" she proclaimed. "You've all done well to make it this far, but if you can't even beat an old woman like me without struggling, I wouldn't dare let you go any further than this. If you think I'm going to let those demons kill yet another group of ignorant youngsters, you're dead wrong."

The fierce determination in her eyes made the resemblance between her and Crow all the clearer; it was exactly what I'd seen in her son's eyes the night he asked me to kill Gram. Still, the way she'd called us ignorant youngsters didn't sit well with me, so for the first time since this conversation-slash-sparring-match had begun, I reached out and caught one of her punches. She gasped, and her attention was entirely focused on me.

"I don't care if you're Crow's mother," I said. "You need to stop running your mouth because you don't know the first thing about us."

We had our own reasons for being on this quest, and our own set of circumstances. Whether we were on the right path, I couldn't say. And I also couldn't begin to guess whether our levels, high as they were, would be a match for the Demon Lord. Meeting Mahiro had made me wonder if his magic circles could be the key to making it back home, but that wasn't a sure thing either. Heck, even if we made it back to our world safe and sound, it was possible time moved at a different rate here, and we'd return to Earth well into the future. Also, and only tangentially related, I had yet to find out what the Level 100 "Special Skill" Commander Saran told me about was.

The more I thought about things, the less I felt I knew. It was possible we weren't on the shortest path to our ultimate destination, but all we could do was try to find our way through the dark and keep pushing forward.

"You guys can bicker about the previous generations all you want," I said, "but me and my teammates have to keep going. If we're not strong enough now, we'll just keep working on it as we go. I appreciate your concern, but it's really not necessary."

While we were here, spinning our tires, my mom's health could be deteriorating. I didn't want to make it home only to find out that my family was gone.

In any event, having said my piece, I let go of Noa's tiny fist.

"Okay, guys! Food's ready!" Hosoyama called out from inside the building.

Oh yeah, I was wondering where the others who weren't sparring had run off to. Guess they were inside making lunch. I couldn't believe it was already past noon, but my stomach was certainly ready for some grub.

"Anyway," I said to Noa, "it seems like you've got the wrong idea, so let me clarify: me and my friends? All we're looking for is a way back to our world. Going to the demon continent is just a stepping stone toward that goal. Maybe we'll end up fighting the demons, or maybe we'll find some sort of middle ground. Who knows?"

If we get through this without any fighting, that'd be swell, but I knew that was a naive hope. I thought back to when we'd first met the Demon Lord's cat servant, and it attacked us in dragon form—it wasn't likely whoever gave orders like those wouldn't cooperate.

"Sorry if you're offended, but we're already short enough on time as it is. And it's not just us—your son is too," I said with finality.

Noa's eyes widened as she realized what I was implying. I could tell from the way he'd fought on our way here—Crow didn't have much time left.

POV: NOA

AS I WATCHED THE BOY garbed in black walk back into the safe house, Gilles walked past me, so I stopped him in order to ask the question plaguing my mind. "What *is* that boy, Gilles?"

I'd known Gilles since he'd lost his mother thanks to my no-good son. At the time, he and I had stood at about the same height. He had long since surpassed me, and his youth was beginning to wane. As a boy, he was a foul-mouthed little brat, but he'd matured a lot. For one who'd lived as long as me, the years and months had passed in the blink of an eye, yet it still moved me to see just how much he'd grown.

"Who do you mean?" asked Gilles, cocking his head.

I pointed at the boy with my chin; a powerful determination lived in him. No mere boy of ten or twenty could have lived a life that would result in such deep-seated resolve, but the way he spoke told me that he was wise beyond his years.

"Ah, yes. Well...I'm not sure I can tell you. The only thing I can say is that Commander Saran took a special interest in him, and as you surmised, he is indeed far stronger than any of us here—the hero Satou included."

I marveled to hear Gilles speak frankly and traced my lips with my forefinger. Gilles recoiled a bit. To be sure, the boy was the only one deft enough to dodge my attacks, and he had arrived several days after the other heroes. Yet he'd done it very naturally and without a hint of malice. If Saran Mithray truly had singled him out from the other summoned heroes, then there must be *something* special about him.

"There aren't many who receive the great Saran Mithray's blessing..."

There must have been something of value in the boy. Maybe he really would be able to succeed where the previous generation had failed. I watched as his black silhouette disappeared into the building; as he stepped through the door, his black eyes caught mine for a split second.

Once he was completely out of sight, I turned to face Gilles. "...So tell me, Gilles. How much longer does that son of mine have?"

It wasn't until the boy had brought it up that I'd even begun to think about my son's life coming to an end. But he was right—the son I knew would have stepped in and stopped me from beating his companions to a pulp. Even if he was confident in their abilities, he was never one to risk his friends coming to unnecessary harm. That was just the type of person my son was. And yet, despite raising his voice at me, he hadn't even attempted to step in and stop me earlier. Or perhaps he wanted to but simply couldn't. At his age, his body probably didn't work like it used to.

Good grief. To think I couldn't even notice such a distinct change in my own son's behavior. I was starting to feel like a senile old woman, in spite of my immortality.

"...If I had to guess, I'd say another year, maybe? But that's assuming he spends it largely at rest, without overexerting himself. If he keeps fighting like he has been lately, then, well..." Gilles trailed off, sounding almost on the verge of tears.

"...I see."

I could only imagine what I must have looked like right then. First, my daughter died young, and now, my son (who I thought had gained immortality like me) was an old man approaching the end of his life. The longer I lived, the more of my loved ones I lost, yet it never got any easier.

"It seems I'm going to be left behind yet again..." I muttered softly.

Gilles must have heard, as he stirred uncomfortably. "I'm sorry you always have to go through these things."

"I-It's fine... Though it sounds like he and I should have a serious chat sooner rather than later, lest I come to regret it."

I had many things I needed to speak to my son about. As a

surviving member of the previous hero's party, I knew he'd come back to this safe house one day, which was why I'd decided to move out here and make it my home base. Never would I have expected to be on such a short time limit.

"I think that's probably for the best, yes," said Gilles.

The only question was whether or not Crow would actually hear me out. Long gone were the days when he'd call me Mama and cling to my skirts. Though one would hope he'd grow out of his rebellious phase by the time he was on his deathbed.

"...May I help you with something?"

After an awkwardly silent lunch, during which I had no opportunity to speak with my son, I wanted to find someplace where I could be alone, so I headed out back. The sudden influx of people over the past few days had left me craving solitude. Figuring the heroes would not want to return to the scene of such carnage anytime soon, I was sure I'd be able to do some thinking alone out there, but it seemed someone else had beaten me to the spot.

It was the girl who'd fallen under the effects of my more powerful bewitchment. The other heroes had been affected by one that caused strife with their companions when they crossed into the forest, and the one she'd fallen under was a subliminal mental imprint that caused her to feel amplified anxiety regarding the person she trusted most—my son. He was the only one around whom she acted strangely. I never expected my son to have much luck with the ladies, given his attitude problems, yet it seemed this girl thought the best of him. I had been interested to see how my bewitchment might affect that, but my son had quickly put the kibosh on my experiment.

When I saw her standing there behind the house, she looked as though she had been waiting for me. It was an awkward situation, as the only one of my son's acquaintances I knew was Gilles, and I had never seen this girl before meeting her in the forest.

"It's a pleasure to meet you. My name is Lia, and I'm a former princess of Uruk."

Her striking cobalt eyes were fixed on me as she curtseyed politely. I knew she had likely not lived an extended life span like my son, yet in some respects, she struck me as far more mature than him. Perhaps that was due to her royal upbringing. However, for whatever reason, hearing her name gave me pause. I recalled my son using her name when he demanded I lift the bewitchment, and though I hadn't felt anything then, something about that name stuck out to me now.

"...What did you say your name was? Lia?"

"Yes. It was Lord Crow who gave me that name, actually."

At this, my eyes widened. True, Lia was a fairly common name, yet it held a special significance in our family. I gasped in disbelief. "My son gave you that name?" I asked.

"Y-yes...? What about it?" she replied, tilting her head in confusion.

I shook my head. Judging from her reaction, she didn't know the significance that name held. The son I knew would have never in a million years thought to name someone that just because they were the child of an honorable or wealthy family. No, there must have been something about this girl. But if he had not seen fit to tell her the name's importance, then it was not my place to do so, and doing so would only make him resent me all the more. We already couldn't hold a conversation without him being sarcastic and flippant.

"Oh, nothing. It's just a fine name, that's all. One that I wouldn't think my son capable of coming up with."

"Thank you. I really like it too."

It seemed like she genuinely felt that way, so I couldn't help but smile. I wondered if *she* felt the same way. "...But I digress. You look as though you have something you wish to say to me. Can I help you with something?" I asked.

If Crow had truly named her Lia, then that made her like something of a granddaughter to me. I couldn't help but feel warmer and more accepting of her than I had been just a moment ago; it might even be enough to get me to open up about things I wouldn't normally.

"Oh, yes. There are a lot of things I'd like to ask you, of course, but most importantly, I just want to know a bit more about Lord Crow."

I nodded, having fully expected that. I'd already witnessed her obsession with my son—carefully watching his every move, trying to anticipate his needs and be of help to him whenever possible, and even bringing his food to him in addition to serving herself. This had seemed odd to me at first, but it must have been their normal rapport, given how the boy in black and his companions didn't seem to find this behavior unusual. My son, too, seemed to just accept it as the norm. Perhaps I had imagined he was digging a figurative moat around himself to keep others out.

"I hope this doesn't come across as too forward or disrespectful, but I was wondering how you feel about Crow's deceased sister after all these years? Your daughter, that is. Are you content to let her memory be worn away by time?"

"What? No, of course not!" I responded instantly, showing far more emotion than I normally would have—but I couldn't help myself. "I assume you've never given birth before, so you probably can't relate to this, but every parent loves the children of their own flesh and blood—even if that child grows up to be a murderer or a seeker of world domination. Even if she was a disobedient child who had the gall to go and die before me, that changes nothing. She is still my *beloved* daughter."

Lia smiled, pleased with this assertion. "Okay, then what about Crow? If the circumstances were flipped and he'd been the one to die instead of her, would you just forget about him and move on?"

"Absolutely not!" I replied without hesitation. Even if I was a little loath to admit it, I couldn't lie. My maternal instincts simply wouldn't let me. "I treasure my kids to this day—my son and daughter both. They're both their father's children, as well as my own. Nothing will ever change that."

I could badmouth him all I liked, but in my heart, my love would always remain the same. I loved my children, and that was all there was to it. After losing their father, and my daughter, the only misery I had left to experience in this world was losing my son to old age. Lia, upon hearing this answer, sighed like a disappointed parent.

"Well, I know your family's business is none of mine, but if that's the case, then you and your son have some serious communication problems you need to work on. I'll have you know that Lord Crow was a nervous wreck from the moment we ran into you in the woods until we made it here."

Apparently, my son's mental state was giving Lia an awful lot of stress. As she told it, he was even oblivious to monsters creeping up on him from behind, forcing his pupil to rush to his aid. She also mentioned how he struggled for well over an hour and wasted countless mana stones trying to start a simple fire. It was at that point I stopped her from saying any more. I had no idea that merely bumping into me would turn my son into a useless mess, though the fact that he was still taking on pupils at this age did surprise me.

"Do you know what Lord Crow said to me the other day? He said that was the first time he'd seen you since he and his sister ran away from home, and you *still* didn't say a word about her. But judging from the fact that you clearly kept in contact with Lord Gilles, it's not as if you haven't been concerned about Lord Crow all these years, is it?"

Despite the shaky foundation for her logic, she had a point. However, I was never one who knew how to say the right thing at the right time. While I was busy trying to keep a close eye on his sister, Crow had gone off and nearly gotten himself killed at the Demon Lord's castle. Then, the moment I started trying to keep a closer eye on him, his sister perished.

"As one who can't die, I've always had all the time in the world. While that might sound like fun for a while, it also means I've had to stand idly by and watch as my family lived out their lives, from start to finish."

And no matter how much I claimed to love them deep down, that didn't change the fact that I was a crotchety old woman who only knew how to complain and criticize. Even here, alone with Lia in a private place, I couldn't bring myself to say the things I truly wished I could tell my son. But Lia couldn't know that, so she simply looked down on me and shook her head as though she were dealing with a stubborn child. She was probably thinking that I was just too proud to admit my feelings, even when Crow wasn't around. And to that I would say: it's none of your business. Still, I wasn't going to just take something like this on the chin, so I decided I'd try to get a little payback.

"You're in love with him, aren't you?" I asked with a wry smirk.

"P-pardon?! No, of course not! A young girl like me could never fall for someone like him! It would be *completely* improper!" So she claimed, yet her beet-red cheeks and squeaky voice failed to convince, and she quickly fled the scene.

My, my, that was an even better reaction than I was hoping for. I was hoping to put the screws to her a little more, actually, but, ah well.

I headed back inside, feeling a little bit better for having spoken with her. Perhaps a girl like her was just the type of person who could rein that son of mine in. I headed back to my room, failing to notice the tail poking out from behind a nearby tree—a tail the *exact* same color as my hair.

My Status as an
Assassin Obviously
Exceeds the Hero's

✦ CHAPTER 4 ✦

Unprepared

POV: MARIA ROSE RETICE

I COULDN'T RECALL when exactly the air inside the castle had started to feel this way.

"Lady Maria? Breakfast is served."

I nodded at my handmaid's words and then followed her toward the dining room. Along the way, I passed by many of the people who lived and worked in the castle, and a young girl around my age who had been brought here via the hero summoning ritual bowed her head to me. I glanced at her briefly before passing by.

The king—my father—had successfully expunged the troublesome hero and that assassin boy from the castle as planned, yet he seemed to be utterly disinterested in any of the other summoned heroes. To him, the only real threats were Saran Mithray, the hero, and the assassin who'd stayed off our radar for nearly a month. We originally hoped we could brainwash the hero and turn him into our puppet, and maybe even use him to kill Saran Mithray, but once he broke the curse, we had no choice but to run him out of the castle. We'd framed the assassin for Saran Mithray's murder so he wouldn't dare come back here ever again.

It was perhaps an oversight on our part that the hero managed to escape with six of his companions, but the fact that he took the only disenchanter in their group was a boon to us. Once we learned her class, we explicitly neglected to give her any specialized instruction and instead strung her along so she wouldn't learn any curse-breaking abilities. And yet, she'd somehow managed to break the hero's curse temporarily anyway.

It seemed the humans from the other world truly were different from us on a fundamental level. Thankfully, she was gone now, so there was no risk of anyone breaking any curses around here anymore. I had been concerned when Saran Mithray had taken a special interest in her, but I assumed she would remember none of his teachings. Nor would she recall her own terrible crime.

I'd brainwashed the summoned heroes still at the castle into thinking they'd been born and raised here and that they were living as simple workers. My handmaids obviously knew the truth, but they would never talk, lest they incur my wrath. Still, I knew they were probably all thinking that this state of affairs could not continue indefinitely. I knew better than to think they were all simply okay with my and my father's deeds, and we had far less in the way of protection than we used to.

After dissolving the knights' regiment, the vice commander, Gilles Asti, left the castle, along with all of the other able-bodied men (or those with half a spine, at least) and we were receiving intel suggesting a portion of the aristocracy was working toward taking matters into their own hands. I really did have to wonder just how long I could keep up this charade.

"What's the matter, Sofia? Do you not like the food?"

"...No, of course I do. It's delicious as always."

As I forced down the flavorless slop, I curled my lips into a smile, and my father smiled back at me with affection he had never shown the real me. I couldn't help but take pity on him though, as he tried so dearly to cling to the traces of my mother that he saw in my face.

My poor, poor old father. After losing my mother, he began to lose touch with the real world, and as I grew older and started looking more and more like my mother, he began calling me by her name and treating me as though I truly was her. He still accomplished his duties as king without issue, and in an official capacity he still recognized me as his daughter as well as a pawn, but when we sat down for meals in private like this, I began to crack.

At first, I simply corrected him each time he mistook me for her, but eventually I realized that thinking I was my mother did an awful lot to stabilize my father's mental state, and so I stopped. In the end, she was the only one he had ever truly loved, and he never spared a stray thought for me, his only daughter. I assumed the only reason he still allowed me in his presence at all was because of my strong resemblance to her—but there was no doubt in my mind that he did not see me as a person.

My father had been in a fairly dire mental state even before we lost my mother. He'd lost his own father and older brothers who were next in line for the throne to an epidemic and had to give up his dream of becoming a painter in order to keep our nation together. It was my mother who supported and rescued his soul during that time. Without her, my father no longer had any reason to cherish or feel affection toward this country and had begun dipping his toe into the dark arts.

"Well, I suppose I'd best get to work," my father said. "Don't worry, my darling. I'll bring you back to life, just you wait. We'll be happy together again soon enough."

"Of course, my king," I said, averting my eyes to avoid the twisted love and desperation oozing from his gaze. "I believe in you."

I felt terrible for my father.

I felt terrible for *myself*.

To bring my mother back to life was to break the basic tenets of life that Eiter the Creator had laid out for us—an unspeakable taboo. If I was being completely honest and truly wished the best for my father, then perhaps I would have killed him the moment he made a deal with the demons. But, in spite of everything, I knew my father was still in there, somewhere deep down, and it was my duty to help him find his peace, no matter the cost.

"I'd follow you all the way to the depths of Hell, Father."

Abnormal though it was, this was the only way I knew to keep us a family.

POV: ???

"I'D FOLLOW YOU all the way to the depths of Hell, Father."

I couldn't help but crack a wicked smile as I listened to the conversation taking place on the other side of the door—it was certainly not your average father-daughter heart-to-heart, *that* was for sure. And yet, it seemed the princess truly believed her family arrangement was perfectly normal and sustainable; it was like she'd been indoctrinated into a cult. The thought gave me goosebumps, and I walked away rubbing my arms as if I were cold.

Ever since the hero summoning ritual, any hint of joviality had been drained from the castle, and an eerie stillness had befallen its halls. This was largely due to the fact that many of the people who once called it home, in addition to the knights, had left in secret, without even letting their families know. How horrible! Yet the king and princess seemed utterly oblivious to the eerie ghost town their castle was becoming—or perhaps they simply felt powerless to stop it. Obviously, the fact that the castle wasn't functioning as normal had had an effect on the common citizenry as well, so it was likely only a matter of time before the nation in its current form collapsed into ruin.

"But I guess that's the whole reason I'm here, now, isn't it?"

My duty was to ensure this country held out until the time was right. No matter how many people left, an entire country would still be fine recompense for our efforts. It fell to me to ensure we could effectively make use of said prize in order to fulfill His Majesty's wishes.

"U-um, excuse me...?"

Just as I was letting myself get lost in thought and considering my next move, someone snuck up and called out to me from behind. I whirled around defensively, only to see a frightened girl staring back at me. One of the princess's handmaids, presumably.

"Can I help you?" I asked.

The castle staff *should* have been informed that I was staying at the castle as an honored guest, and most of them treated me as such as evidenced by the lack of suspicion with which I was viewed. However, this girl looked upon me with a mixture of fear and suspicion, and I could think of any number of reasons for that. Yes, it was truly annoying having all these humans scurrying around like insects. I couldn't know what this girl had seen, of course, but she had certainly caught me doing *something*. I clicked my tongue in frustration at my own negligence.

"What did you do to her... Where's Ange?! I saw you with her yesterday, but the moment you touched her, she disappeared! I searched the entire castle and couldn't find her. Where did you take her? Where...?" the girl asked me, her tone tentative at first, but then reassured.

I blinked a few times in disbelief, but then burst out in laughter. "Pfft... *Bwa ha ha ha ha ha!*"

The girl grimaced in discomfort as I doubled over laughing, and she took a step back. I moved forward, close enough to reach out and touch the girl. The girl, having no fighting experience, was helpless to do anything as I grabbed her.

"My, you humans truly are a delight. Such foolish, simple-minded creatures—you really are beyond saving," I said, my voice ringing throughout the empty corridor. If this had been only a few days earlier, there would have been all sorts of onlookers to see this, but now there were none. But of course, there were none—they'd all "gone away," after all.

"But," I continued, "you saw me yesterday, did you? That was a blunder on my part. I know! As a reward for your observation, why don't I let you go see your friend again? What did you say her name was? *Ange?*" I reached into my breast pocket and pulled out a tiny stone.

"W-wait, so you *do* know where she is?! Then tell me! Where's Ange?!"

The girl was screaming hysterically now, twisting her body back and forth in an attempt to wrest her arm free from my grasp, but I held on tight. I tilted my head curiously and held the small stone up in front of her eyes so that she could take a long, hard look at it.

"Take a good look, my dear. *This* is the girl you've been searching for," I said, and the girl immediately seized up, her lips trembling. "You humans hold surprisingly little value in the grand scheme of things, you know. Your entire lives only hold about as much value as a pebble by the side of the road. Though I guess you can't help it, since none of you have even a tiny fraction of the mana *we* do."

"W-wait, you're...you're a demon?! How did a demon get into the castle?! Someone, he—!!!"

The girl, having finally realized my true identity, tried to cry out for help but disappeared in the next instant. I opened the hand with which I'd been grasping her arm to find a tiny stone resting in my palm, which hadn't been there a moment ago.

"So...all your life amounted to was a tiny pebble as well, eh? How utterly dull."

I took both it and the other stone in one hand and tossed them across the hall. There was no value in holding on to such worthless things. The human race was far more pitiful than I ever could have thought.

With my Equivalent Exchange skill, I had the ability to convert things into other things which held the same predetermined value: I didn't pick the value. I knew this because I once tried converting someone I cared for quite deeply and ended up with only a small jewel in exchange, whereas another time I converted someone who I was not the least bit interested in and got back a lovely tiara encrusted with giant gemstones. So regrettably, my personal opinion didn't factor into the equation.

As His Majesty told it, the one who determined these things was the god of this world—Eiter. I didn't believe in any god, but I did acknowledge that whoever was deciding the values of things couldn't be a mere mortal. There was no way any mortal would have decided that individuals of their race were worth nothing more than mere gemstones.

I couldn't help but pity the humans, in a way. I wondered what it felt like to have your life amount to nothing more than a *pebble*. And yet, they lived with such fierce passion for life and all its wonders—the poor things. It was almost cute how hard they tried despite the futility of it all. Yes, how very entertaining.

"I've grown quite tired of these tiny rocks. Hopefully I can at least find *something* around here that I can exchange for, I don't know...a flower, maybe?"

The only sound that remained in the now-empty hallway was my own footsteps. I wondered how much value this entire country held in total. *I know! Since I still need to kill time until His Majesty gives the signal, why don't I go see how much value those summoned heroes have? That ought to make the time go by faster, at least.*

POV: SATOU TSUKASA

"THERE'S SOMETHING I need to tell you."

Akira's arrival marked the end of Noa using us as punching bags. I wasn't sure if that was because his words of protest had resonated with her or if she'd just been toying with the rest of us from the outset. I had never been any good at telling how people truly felt. The world would be a much simpler place if everyone's minds worked via the same simple thought processes.

The day after Akira arrived was a warm and sunny, and I was struggling to keep myself from dozing off as I cleaned the windows. Suddenly, Noa appeared in front of me and, with a straight face (and after ensuring no one else was around) told me she had something she needed to tell me. After yesterday, this immediately put me on guard, but then I remembered that she'd never attacked any of us except when we were braced and ready. Perhaps that was her way of being considerate as she pounded us into shape, brutal though it was.

"...And what might that be?" I replied, wringing out my cloth before throwing it into the water bucket. I stood up and looked down on the pint-sized pulverizer, whose eyes were fixed on my sword as she shoved me into a dark corner where no one else could see us. "Got something to say about my sword?"

It was the sturdy blade I'd received at the castle, where I was told it was a holy sword. It had saved my bacon countless times along our journey, and I was so used to it by now that I almost considered it a fifth limb. Which made it all the more frustrating that I was beginning to doubt its "holy" powers. No matter how much I practiced, I couldn't seem to use any holy sword techniques on command. But imagine if I could use those skill *all* the time, and how much easier this all would be—the thought kept me up at night.

"I see your blade has not become the holy sword as of yet," she said.

The word "yet" stuck out like a sore thumb, and I put my hand on the blade's hilt instinctively. But the girl simply traced her lips with her fingers, not bothered by me standing ready to draw my blade.

"The holy sword does not simply get passed down from generation to generation of heroes, you see—that would be much too simple. Some say 'the holy sword' refers to one specific blade meant for the hero's use, but that's a common misconception.

One does not simply inherit the holy sword. When one with the class of hero picks up a weapon—any weapon—and forms a strong enough bond with it...only then does it grant the hero the power of the holy sword. It's a good thing it's not always a sword too; otherwise, it would be quite awkward for those with especially massive or puny builds to wield, no?"

My eyes widened as she explained all of this. I suppose I had fallen into the trap of assuming the holy sword was something of this world's Excalibur, which only the chosen hero could wield. But now that I thought about it more, I realized that after my first sword broke down in the labyrinth and they gave me my current one, it hadn't felt awkward at all, not until I'd started questioning whether or not it was actually the holy sword. I ran my hand along its all-too-familiar hilt as I looked down at Noa.

"...And you're sure that's how it works?" I asked.

Even if what she was saying was true, I found it hard to believe, coming from someone so antagonistic. Sure, she seemed like she was being genuine, but it was impossible to know where her true motivations lay. I also couldn't help thinking about when we'd been deceived by people pretending to be timid back in Mali.

"...Well, obviously I can't say so with one hundred percent certainty. Most people are lucky to meet even a single hero in their lifetimes, after all. Even I, as long as I've lived, have only laid eyes upon two," she said, smiling as she slowly stepped back toward the building. "Let me just give you one piece of wisdom passed down from your predecessor: 'A hero's ability to awaken the holy sword depends entirely on the hero's own experience, and the strength of his heart.' You're free to believe them or not, but do try to keep them in mind."

With that, Noa disappeared into the shadow of the building. I'd been trying very hard to figure out how to use the holy sword technique again over the past few days but had given up, assuming I had the wrong sword—not the wrong state of mind. My sword was fine as any, and it had weathered our long and arduous journey without even a crack.

"...Could it be that you've already accepted me as your wielder, old pal?"

I pulled the sword from its sheath a bit, and the sun reflected brilliantly off the blade. For just a split second, the blade shimmered brightly, almost as if it were answering my question.

POV: ODA AKIRA

HAVING FINALLY ARRIVED at our destination, I needed three whole days to heal the wounds from our journey and fully recover my strength. The forest had been about as dangerous as the lowest levels of any labyrinth, and the monsters really did seem to get stronger the closer we got to demon country.

The six of us now sat where Crow and his companions had, back when he'd lived here. Noa, who I assumed owned the house, stood directly behind Crow; Amaryllis and Lia, who hadn't met the other heroes, introduced themselves before standing behind us (though Amaryllis was half-hiding behind Lia). I could tell that Noa, despite often referring to Crow as her "worthless son," watched him with motherly concern. She was an enigma I couldn't quite nail down.

"So, is there an easy way into the demon continent?" I asked Crow and Noa, resting an elbow on the table. There must have been *some* route nearby as the previous hero generation had used this place as its forward base of operations, but many decades had passed since then and things could have changed. Crow and Noa had left two days ago to scout the area, but judging from the looks on their faces, things weren't looking good.

"From what we could tell, the secret undersea tunnels we used all those years ago have been rendered impassable due to cave-ins and flooding and whatnot," Crow declared, and despair fell over the heroes' faces. But that wasn't even the end of the bad news Crow had to share. "We can't go by boat either, because the monsters living in that part of the ocean are far too dangerous. We also were able to learn our secret tunnel didn't collapse due to natural causes. Though faint, we did find traces of mana having been used in the vicinity a while ago."

"...So what does that mean?" inquired Waki, ignoring the little cat and monkey pulling at his hair.

"It means the demons did it intentionally, and they probably sent one of their strongest guys to do the job—someone with enough power to cause an artificial cave-in that looked indistinguishable from a natural disaster."

The demons were expecting us then. Crow used a map to show us the destroyed pathways. As he spoke, I zoned out, and the faces of demons, like Mahiro and Aurum, we'd encountered in the Great Labyrinth of Brute popped into my mind. I had no doubt either of them could have caused the same level of destruction as a natural disaster, no problem.

"The routes from here to the elven domain and human continent are still open. It's only the paths directly into demon territory that have conveniently caved in, eh?"

Surprisingly, the previous generation of heroes had constructed underground tunnels not only into the demons' territory but also to each of the other continents as well. Making a secret passageway into enemy territory made sense to me, especially since it wasn't that far from here geographically, but digging out tunnels to every corner of the world seemed overly cautious and like a lot of extra work. Obviously, Crow had traveled with the heroes at the time and would know more about their motives, but it seemed like he'd deferred to their judgment most of the time. It was hard to say for sure though.

"How hard would it be to make those tunnels passable again?" asked the hero, raising his hand.

Both Crow and his mother shook their heads. "Not happening. They're in an extremely poor state. Moving even a single piece of rubble could cause further collapse," said Noa, nipping that idea right in the bud. A heavy silence fell over the room.

"So...we can't go by sea and we can't go underground, either," muttered the hero, clearly disheartened by these revelations. I felt the same way, but I said nothing and kept staring at Noa. Out of the corner of my eye, I could see Amelia doing the same.

"...If you've got any better ideas, I'm all ears," said Noa with a sigh, caving to the pressure of our combined gazes.

Amelia and I glanced at one another, and then I voiced the first idea that had come to my mind: "...W-why don't we go by air?"

"That's it!" said the hero, clapping his hands. "If we can't walk, we can just *fly* there!"

All of us summoned heroes who were used to the idea of airplanes immediately brightened up at this idea, whereas the trueborn Morriganites were clearly a bit lost. The hero proceeded to explain airplanes and how they worked in simple terms. Unfortunately, I wasn't able to follow any of it, which made me feel a little pathetic. All the stuff he was saying about "airspeed velocity" and "aerodynamic lift" and how they related to "runway length" and "takeoff velocity" was complete gibberish to me. Maybe I was destined to be a liberal arts major.

Crow seemed equally confused as he began to zone out, but Noa was downright captivated and started throwing all manner of questions the hero's way. They were mother and child, and yet they couldn't be more different.

"I see. Yes...flight through the air *does* seem theoretically possible," she finally declared with a nod, having probed the full extent of the hero's knowledge on the subject. Meanwhile, the rest of us who weren't able to follow their conversation were looking off in different directions. Kyousuke seemed to be completely dissociating, standing there with his eyes closed.

"But just to clarify, I'm not an expert on the subject! I couldn't tell you any of the mathematics behind it!" the hero said, waving his hands back and forth as if to say it wasn't his fault if this got us all killed.

"Well, I suspect their reason for suggesting going by air lies with me," said Noa. "Isn't that right, Amelia Rosequartz and Akira Oda?"

Amelia and I both sat up straight as if we'd just been cracked by a whip. We both nodded, each of us having gotten the idea from a certain part of Noa's stat page. If we could borrow her abilities, I had a feeling flying was a viable option. Having come to an agreement, we quickly began discussing what she would need to make it happen.

"Okay, I think we should start by splitting into teams."

According to Noa, we'd need to gather a fair number of raw materials in order to make our plan work, so obtaining those was our first priority. We'd need to head back into the forest to get them, but it didn't make sense to move as one big group, so I suggested we split up to make things easier, and everyone else agreed. Including myself, there were now thirteen of us—fourteen if you included Night, who wasn't here currently—so we could split into three solid teams fairly easily.

"Well, first off, I think Amelia, Amaryllis, and the noncombatants should stay here and hold down the fort. And you too, of course," I said to Noa, to which she huffed as if to say she didn't need me to tell her that.

"Wait, you want me to stay behind?" asked Amelia, crestfallen.

She could tell I was trying to keep her out of the fighting as much as possible, but I'd had a feeling she'd react like this, and

I gave her the answer I'd prepared in advance: "I need you and Noa to stay here to defend the others and the house. We'd be in deep trouble if we lost our home base," I said, plopping my hand atop her head reassuringly. She smiled shyly, then nodded. I had a feeling that Noa could defend the house all by herself.

"The others and I are going to work together to gather all of the resources Noa laid out for us—or at least the closest things we can find," I went on. "Let's have one team serve as the battle unit that'll go out and fight monsters to collect materials, and the other team go scout the tunnel the previous hero generation used to see if there's anything there we can salvage."

At the very least, I knew that the hero, Kyousuke, Gilles, and I needed to be in the battle unit. Tsuda and Lia, with their shield and barriers, should probably go along with Crow and the others to protect them while they gathered and appraised materials from the underground passage—and they should also take Night in case they had to make a quick getaway. The battle unit would have fewer people than the other team, but none of us had been in combat together before, so fewer people would be safer. Worst-case scenario, I could fend for myself and the other three, who had traveled together through the forest, would be fine.

"Okay. Battle unit, we'll be heading out as soon as we're done doing maintenance on our equipment. It'd be great if the rest of you could wait here until Night arrives," I said.

"Yeah, what about that furball? Haven't seen him once since we entered the forest," Crow grumbled. Judging from all the nodding, Amaryllis was the only one who hadn't noticed

Night's absence. She was, for better or worse, an ordinary girl who happened to know a lot about medicine and was just along for the ride.

"Yeah, so…Night's coming via a different route. He's fulfilling a request from Amaryllis."

I looked over at her, only to find that she'd hidden herself behind Lia to escape the curious glances. Having no other choice, I told everyone the story of how she'd won the beauty pageant years ago and then was kidnapped and forced to make drugs for a beastfolk man named Gram. Gram fed the drugs to his personal retinue of mercenaries and exported them with some of them making it to the human continent to be taken by the assassins that killed Commander Saran. As soon as I finished explaining, Ueno's face went deathly pale, and I wondered why she reacted so strongly.

I decided to keep that question to myself for the time being.

"I brought Amaryllis along with us so she could develop an antidote to the effects of that drug, which is still out there in pretty large quantities. In order to do that, she needs some herbs that grow a fair bit west of here, so I sent Night to collect some. It might take a while, though, so hopefully Hosoyama and the others can teach Amaryllis a few things while you guys are posted here."

I cast a quick glance over at Amaryllis, who was still trembling behind Lia, then looked over at the members of my team, who were checking their equipment. "You gonna be ready to head out soon?"

"Natch. How 'bout yourself?"

I couldn't help but snort at the hero trying to be smart with me but drew my dual daggers—each a half of the blade that had once been the Yato-no-Kami. "I don't have to 'get' ready. I'm *always* ready."

Always ready because, as I learned early on down in the labyrinth, monsters weren't gonna wait for you to be prepared to fight back.

POV: TSUDA TOMOYA

"GOD, THIS PLACE IS A MESS..." Crow muttered as he looked at the collapsed tunnel which had once connected the beast-folk continent to the demon continent.

I couldn't imagine how many hours of grueling work it must have taken to dig it out, and how it must feel for him to see all that work crumbled to dust. There were pungent traces of mana in the air, telling even an amateur like me that there had, indeed, been demons at work here.

"There's no time to be sad about it. Is there anything here we can use?" asked Night, looking around at the mana stones lighting the tunnel and the strangely colored ores lining the cave walls.

Night had arrived in house-cat form shortly after the battle unit had departed. When Amaryllis saw the medicinal herbs he'd brought with him, she made a face I'd rather not recall. It was hard to believe someone with looks like hers was capable of drooling over a pile of *plants*. Even Night seemed taken aback, and honestly, I found it hard to watch.

"...Looks like we can still use the mana stones and ores. I can sense a little bit of mana in them. Everything over here's no good, though..." said Crow despondently, as though he were truly heartbroken. I could only imagine how much he respected the previous generation of heroes; he probably felt a lot more connected to them than he did us, despite being heroes ourselves. "Aoi...Luke...Ritter..." he muttered repeatedly to himself as he went through the wreckage. At first, I thought it was some sort of chant, but then I realized they were names.

"So, these and those, eh? Great. Now let's get out of here before this place collapses further. Come on, Crow. Let's move on to the next area," said Night.

I could almost hear the sound of the tension snapping in my brain. *How can one cat be so bad at reading the room? Clearly Oda's rubbing off on him, and in a seriously bad way.* I walked up behind the black cat and grabbed him by the scruff of his neck, holding him in front of my face. Despite being a monster, he was still a cat, and like with any feline, this rendered him completely motionless.

"Hey, what's this all about?! Let me go!"

I gave Lia a signal with my eyes, then left the two of them behind as I carried Night back above ground with me. With Lia's barriers, she could probably protect the others without my help.

"Hey! I told you to let me go!!!" Night enlarged himself briefly to escape my grasp and then shrank back down before landing on the ground and glaring up at me intimidatingly, just like the cat at my grandma's house back home. *"What is the meaning of this?!"* he hissed.

I towered over him imposingly. "Are you completely emotionless, or *what*?! Did you seriously not feel a thing seeing Crow all broken up like that?"

"Of course I'm sympathetic to him, but if we keep dragging our feet like this, it'll take days to get through all of these spots! You know I'm right, don't you?"

He did have a point—if Crow was going to have an emotional breakdown at each and every place we stopped at, there was no way we'd be back before sundown. There were just too many tunnels to check, and all of them were dangerous. If we wasted too much time, it was very likely more routes would collapse and become impassable to us. But I didn't want to admit that, so I shook my head like a child having a temper tantrum.

"No, you don't get it! You...just don't get it. Maybe a monster like you wouldn't understand what it's like to lose a friend or loved one, but not everyone can just man up and be unaffected by the thought of having lost someone forever! And Crow's lost *way* more people who were important to him than any of us, and many of us would be an absolute mess after losing just one!" I knew it wasn't my place to speak on his behalf, especially since I'd never lost anyone truly close to me, but I couldn't just stand by, so I was screaming at Night with more passion than I had screamed at anyone in my life.

"*...I have no right to act considerately toward him,*" said Night, as I panted for breath and glared down at him. He responded to me plainly, without averting his eyes. "*Did I ever tell you that it* *was the Demon Lord himself who breathed life into me? That for years, I worked as his most faithful servant?"*

I had heard an awful lot about Night during our discussions with himself, Crow, and Amelia as we'd waited for Oda to regain consciousness back at Crow's house in Ur. At the time, I was just amused to see that there were talking cats amongst the monsters of this world, so most of his words had gone in one ear and out the other.

"When Crow and the previous hero arrived at His Majesty's castle, fully prepared to die, I stood at His Majesty's side, both in order to protect him and to help him escape if worst came to worst. In the end, the heroes were bested by his second-in-command right outside the throne room, and then escaped while I and the other demons laughed and ridiculed them."

I held my breath as Night quietly told his story. It was hard to believe the tiny cat who spent most of his time on Oda's shoulders had once done such a thing. I didn't know what went down before he met Oda, or how he'd joined Oda, but I'd assumed he was an underling, not the Demon Lord's right-hand monster.

"And then there was the whole 'Nightmare of Adorea' debacle. That was when Gram forced Crow's sister off of an escape boat, and she was subsequently crushed beneath a falling building. The 'nightmare' that led to the collapse was a rampage conducted by me on His Majesty's orders. Something which I did happily in the hopes of earning His favor."

I hadn't seen Night fight before, though I remembered Amelia boasting about how he transformed himself into a giant dragon when they first fought him. I could only imagine what that must have looked like, since I hadn't been there. Night carried on explaining his laundry list of evil deeds, regardless of my reaction.

"I did regret that later, after seeing the stone monument they erected for the victims, but until that point, I genuinely did not believe I'd done anything wrong, nor did I care how much damage I'd done or how many lives I'd extinguished."

Suddenly, his golden eyes were staring right through me, and my body stiffened up. I felt no malice, nor was I under the effects of any spell, and yet I was completely unable to move from beneath that gaze.

"Do you get it now? I'm both directly and indirectly responsible for the deaths of virtually everyone who was ever important to him. Do you really think he'd appreciate their murderer trying to offer his condolences? I let Master and Lady Lia take care of that," he muttered, then headed back underground with his tail hung low.

I stood there unable to move for a good while after he left. It was the first time I'd ever managed to really give someone a piece of my mind, and yet I didn't feel satisfied at all.

"...Man, why's this stuff gotta be so hard?"

I never had so much trouble finding the right words back in my world. The blue sky above was warm and clear, in direct contrast to what I now felt in my heart.

We checked five more caved-in tunnels, one of which was fully collapsed, so we needed Night to shrink down and check it out for us, though all he managed to bring back was a single, worn-out notebook. Its pages were yellowed and brittle. The cover might have once been red, but it was honestly hard to tell. Crow cocked his head at the sight of it, apparently having no memory of the notebook, but we didn't have time to stand around reading through it, so I simply tossed it in my bag with the few mana stones I was carrying.

"Okay, how many more spots do we have to check?"

Night looked up at Crow as he walked down the corridor, allowing him to answer. He looked down at Night with listless, sunken eyes. "All that's left now is the base camp we made for ourselves while we were working on the tunnels. That's where we made the mana stone devices we used in all of the tunnels. There should definitely be something usable there."

Crow started walking outside at a brisk pace, and we all hurried to keep up. Seeing the tunnels and the work that had gone into them made it plainly evident just how incredible the previous generation of heroes had been. I couldn't imagine how many hours of work had gone into making the tunnels, even just the one to the demon continent: especially when they'd had families and places they belonged, unlike us, who were all just focused on taking down the Demon Lord.

I had to wonder how we would have managed in a scenario like theirs. After all, it's not as though they had Noa or any previous heroes around to point them in the right direction. I wondered if we could have done what they did in a situation like that. *Yeah, no way in hell*, I thought, scoffing sarcastically to myself as

I followed after Night and Crow. We arrived at the camp Crow described before too long which made sense, given that it was right where they started the first tunnel.

"Here we are," he said.

It was a small building, perfectly hidden behind some trees, though it was worn enough to look a bit like ruins. It was the sort of place a group of kids would be thrilled to find and make into their secret hideout.

"Wow, I'm surprised you were able to still find this old place," Night snorted upon first sight of it.

"Yeah, well. Lotta good memories here," Crow muttered under his breath.

I could sense the place was drawing up a lot of feelings for the old man, and I didn't really know whether or not me saying anything would be appropriate.

"Whoa!"

As soon as we entered the hidden doorway to the building, Lia cried out in amazement. The walls were all done up in bright colors, and the interior was far neater and tidier than one ever would have expected from the outside.

"My, would you look at that..." marveled Night, looking at a strange device covered in dust and illuminated by the light seeping in.

"Wouldn't touch that if I were you. You might just lose a limb," warned Crow in a threatening manner, and Night quickly drew back his outstretched paw.

I had no idea what the dust-covered appliance might be, but that only made me more curious about what it did.

"We didn't leave many dangerous things laying around, but some stuff could be more dangerous now. Be careful," he said with narrowed eyes, a hint of longing in his voice.

The previous hero's party had consisted of four people, one from each of the world's continents (aside from Volcano). The only two who survived their quest were the hero and Crow, though the hero was long dead by now, so only Crow remained. Having a far longer life span than anyone else he knew, Crow surely had to stand by and watch as the majority of his friends died off and left him behind. I couldn't even imagine what that must feel like.

As I was lost in thought, I didn't notice Crow walk right up to me. Panicked, I quickly moved out of the way, but my leg caught on something, and I tripped. I reached out to grab something and catch myself, and my hands landed on something dusty.

"Uh-oh."

It was the thing Crow had warned us not to touch. I'd been standing next to it in the hopes I'd have a chance to satisfy my curiosity about it, but it seemed that plan had backfired. I froze, and Crow's gaze shot over to the device, which was now rattling with some sort of mana.

"Hey! Let go of that, you idiot!" he barked, ripping my hands away in a hurry. A moment later, the device gave off a bright light, filling the room. Crow and I, being right next to it, had to shield our eyes from the brightness.

"...What *was* that?" Crow whispered as the light finally abated. Apparently, he didn't know exactly what the thing did either.

"Hey! Who goes there?!" Night growled, peering through the cloud of dusty smoke that filled the room.

"What the..."

Standing in the middle of the room was a man and a woman who had not been there when we entered. And though I used the word "standing," their bodies were decidedly transparent. The word "ghosts" came to mind. Crow was still holding my arm, and I could feel his hands begin to tremble.

"You seem well, Crow."

"Long time no see, big brother!"

POV: CROW

"Wha..."

...The sound leaked out from between my lips like a measured breath.

"What's the matter, man? Ain't never seen you make a face like that before."

He smiled at me with the same smile I remembered—yet one that should no longer exist in this world. The black panther beastfolk who'd been heralded as the hero, and who had been my best friend from childhood, who meant more to me than anyone except for my little sister.

"Ritter...? Is that *you*?" I asked, gazing upon him in disbelief. I quickly shook my head, sure I was seeing things. "No, that can't be. You died a long time ago, and I didn't even get to be by your deathbed. If only I could have been there..."

I remembered it well. I'd been experiencing an influx of orders at the time and life had gotten in the way, so I hadn't even found out that my best friend had died until two weeks after he was already gone. I really was an asshole—only ever thinking about myself, never checking in with anyone else. I was always too late when it mattered most: I couldn't get there in time when my sister died, and I didn't get to say goodbye to my best friend. There was always something getting in the way, preventing me from moving forward.

"*Wow, big brother! Sounds like you've turned into a real softie,*" giggled the girl, her hand over her mouth. This was the "polite" way to laugh that my mother had drilled into her.

"*...Alia.*"

The girl bore the same face, the same expression, and even had the same way of laughing as the little sister of my memories. My chest tightened looking at that face—one I hadn't seen in so very, very long.

Not long after she died, a baby was born in a small village I just happened to be passing through. Having lost both my best friend and my little sister, I was wandering around looking for a place to die, when I encountered a baby girl who gave me a reason to live again. Her mother's name was Lilia. She was a beautiful woman, but tragically lost her life in a monster attack just after her daughter was born.

Once again, I was too late to help, for I was out picking medicinal herbs at the time. And so it was then that I gave the girl the name Lia, after all of the women I most respected—Alia, Lilia, Amelia. In all honesty, I had been hoping to raise her as a replacement for my deceased sister, which was the main reason for the name. Of course, that stubborn tomboy Lia could never truly replace my dear sister.

"I...I...I don't deserve to see either of you again..." I stuttered. I still didn't understand how they could be here, but I would never mistake my own sister. She was the real deal, and I fell straight back into my old speaking patterns.

Amused, Alia simply giggled again.

"Nah, c'mon! He's always been a big softie at heart, you know that?" teased Ritter, placing his transparent hand on Alia's transparent shoulder.

Behind me, I could hear Tsuda gasping "They're *ghosts*?!" He was probably not too far off, to be fair.

"I see... This device must use some sort of necromancy to call back the souls of lost loved ones for whoever charges it with mana," I posited. It must have been an extremely complicated magical device, one I could neither make nor repair at my current age. I wiped the dust off the device and sighed. It seemed my old friend's inventing capabilities had surpassed mine, even back when he was still alive. And they still worked better than anything I had ever made. No wonder he was chosen to be the hero.

"That's correct. I'm guessing that boy there who touched it hasn't lost any loved ones since coming of age, so the device simply used him

as a conduit and channeled the mana of the next closest person, and now, here we are."

I looked at Ritter, smiling smugly. Just looking at his soft, friendly expression was enough to get me all choked up.

"Yeah, right. Don't pretend like you didn't design that thing with me in mind," I said. It had been many years since I last set foot in this room, so my memory was a little fuzzy, but I knew there had been no device here when I left. "I left all sorts of stuff here, so you knew I'd be back eventually. I bet you just wanted to mess with me when I came back, didn't you? You probably put it here after we came back from the Demon Lord's castle."

He was always very meticulous and crafty like that. Yet as I let out a heavy sigh, Ritter's gaze wandered to the other members of my party before ultimately settling on one in particular. *"By the way...is that the infamous Black Cat you're walking around with?"* Ritter asked, looking down at Night with a twinkle in his eye.

Come to think of it, we had been about to make our way to the Demon Lord's castle when we first heard the rumors about his right-hand monster.

"That's right. Though right now he's an ally of the current generation of heroes," I replied, and Ritter immediately burst out laughing. I'd forgotten just how little it took to crack him up.

"You gotta be kidding me! The Demon Lord's most loyal servant, now a turncoat?!" he howled, clutching his belly with both hands, and Alia couldn't help but join in too.

I sighed and shook my head. I could barely get a word in edgewise with this guy—he simply steered the conversation however he saw fit. "Enough about that. Why did you leave this magic device behind for me in the first place?" I asked. Surely if he'd gone out of his way to construct *something* and leave it here, he must have had something he needed to tell me.

POV: LIA LAGOON

"WHY DID YOU LEAVE this magic device behind for me in the first place?" asked Crow, and even I could feel the sudden tension.

It was foreboding enough that I actually started lifting my staff to cast a barrier purely by reflex. Tsuda, too, raised his shield a little bit from behind Lord Crow. Night didn't seem particularly on guard, but judging from his stance, he did seem a little tense, consciously or otherwise.

"Aw, c'mon. Can't we at least enjoy our long-awaited reunion a little more before we get into that?" said the previous hero, smiling broadly as though he didn't notice the tension in the air.

I honestly wasn't sure whether to judge him for being unable to read the room, or if it was just the dauntlessness of a true hero shining through.

Lady Alia, at least, seemed to see how uncomfortable we all were, and let out a sigh. *"Jeez, Ritter. You really haven't changed, even in death... You've really gotta learn how to read the room..."* she said, looking first at Ritter, then at me, then Night, then Tsuda.

"I apologize, you guys, but could we give my brother and Ritter some privacy, please? Besides, there's something unrelated I'd like to ask you. I hope you'll hear me out."

We all looked at each other, then nodded. To be honest, I didn't want to stay in the middle of the awkward situation even a second longer. Lady Alia smiled, relieved that we were agreeable to her suggestion. Weirdly enough, her warm smile reminded me a little bit of the peaceful look on Lord Crow's face whenever he was fast asleep.

"Thank you, I appreciate that... We've been watching you all for quite some time, though mostly just my brother. I believe we have a rough idea of your current circumstances. Also, Night, if you could call the current hero, and Tsuda, if you could call our mother, Noa, here, that would be much appreciated. We should be able to stay manifested in this world for about a day, but I can't promise any longer than that. Please, do hurry if you can."

After hearing Lady Alia's request, Night and Tsuda immediately nodded and headed for the door. She then turned to me and smiled playfully. *"In the meantime, why don't you and I have a little chat, Lia? I only ever had my brother, obviously, but I always wanted a sister."*

With her voice clear as crystal as she smiled from ear to ear, I could hardly say no. If she had truly been watching over us for so long, then surely she knew about the feelings I harbored for Lord Crow. I nodded, resigned to my fate, and her smile grew even wider.

As sparks seemed to be flying between the previous hero and Lord Crow, the two of us decided to move into the lounge next door in order to escape the uncomfortable atmosphere. The room itself was quite dusty, but the seats we sat on were much less so, even if they weren't perfectly clean. It was, perhaps, the ideal environment to have a discussion with the dead.

"Tee hee... You don't have to be so on edge, you know. Even if I did want to hurt you, we have no power to intervene in the world of the living. Let's just have a casual chat until my mother arrives, shall we?"

The way she covered her mouth with her hand when she laughed was more elegant and refined than half of the royals back in the palace. I couldn't imagine Lord Crow would have insisted on teaching her such a thing, so it must have been Lady Noa's doing. Her facial structure itself was every bit as perfect as Lord Crow's, and it even made me start to wonder if she was secretly of royal blood herself.

"...What would you like to talk about?" I asked. We had no tea or cakes to dine on, as the only thing on the coffee table between us was a thick layer of dust. Not that this felt like much of a tea party anyway.

"Oh, come now, there's no need to be so guarded. I really just want to talk to you...as my future sister-in-law, of course."

My heart skipped a couple beats, and then my mouth hung wide open. I was so baffled by the words that I didn't even care that I probably looked like a slack-jawed idiot.

"Y-your...sister-in-law?" I replied, struggling to even get the words out.

"I mean, you're going to marry my brother, aren't you?"

"BWHAAA?!"

POV: ODA AKIRA

"HEY, HERO! It's headed your way! Look alive!!!" I yelled at the hero, who was gasping for breath on his knees.

"Don't...b-boss me around!" he cried out in irritation as he picked himself up.

I didn't remember him being so useless. I couldn't help but shake my head. This was our first time fighting side by side. Down in the Great Labyrinth of Kantinen, he had been on the front lines while I brought up the rear, until that minotaur showed up and our positions flipped after he broke both his arms.

"Kyousuke! Be careful not to damage its tusks! They're the materials we need!"

"Yes, I'm...well *aware*!!!"

The hero, Kyousuke, Gilles, and I were currently gathering the necessary resources Noa requested so that we could cross to the other continent. Anything close to the safe house that wasn't monster-related would be gathered by Amaryllis and Amelia while we were gone, whereas those of us in the battle unit were specifically looking for monster materials. But it wasn't proving to be all that easy.

This forest was as close to demon territory as it got, which meant the monsters here were stronger than even those on the lowest levels of any labyrinth. And a group of large boar-headed monsters were swarming us right now. In true boar fashion, they'd charged at us the moment we set foot on their territory, making a reckless beeline right for us. If we were skewered by their tusks, we'd be done for.

I dodged one, and it charged straight into a giant tree behind me, getting its tusks stuck. The tree was ripped out of the ground by its roots due to the impact, but it remained attached to the beast's tusks. The beast shook its head back and forth to get free, then turned to look at me again. I had to admire its neck strength, necessary for it to skewer its prey. Thankfully, I was quick enough to dodge its charges, but I was worried whether my other party members could do the same.

"Akira! We'll draw its attention and create an opportunity for you, so you just focus on chopping its head off!" yelled Gilles.

As a former vice knight commander, he was far better at doling out orders than I was. Night and Amelia usually did exactly as I wanted them to without me having to ask, so I hadn't had to really work to operate as part of a team since leaving the castle. That was probably why Gilles had asked me to be the one to deal the finishing blow—because he knew I was a lone wolf.

"You got it!" I replied, then used Conceal Presence. Now that I didn't have to worry about working with anyone, there was no need for me to remain visible. Quickly, the hero, Kyousuke, and Gilles drove the monster into a more densely wooded area where trees would obstruct its path. Now it was my turn. "Shadow Magic, activate... Shadow Lattice!"

Our shadows, and the shadows of the trees around us, all congregated to draw a lattice pattern beneath the monster's feet. A monster of its size would normally be enough to feed all of us for several days, but we had no need of its meat now that we had a base camp to go back to, so I had no qualms about dicing the monster up into tiny pieces. When the shadows were done, all that remained was a fleshy lump.

"Hey! What about the tusks...?!" the hero cried out in a fluster, but he quickly shut up the moment I reappeared, tusks in hand.

Obviously, I wasn't going to forget about our main objective. I'd ripped them off before I even used my Shadow Magic. As soon as the battle was over and I verified there were no other monsters nearby, we took a break. The pungent scent of blood and death permeated the air, probably made worse by the fact that I'd diced the monster into pieces. It would be best to get out of here ASAP.

I broke off some bark from a nearby tree and used it to scrape the blood off my daggers. I would have preferred to simply wipe it off with a soft cloth, but we'd brought no such dead weight item along with us, and I wouldn't want to have to walk around with a blood-soaked cloth afterward anyway. This meant my only real options were to use tree bark, or wait until a humanoid enemy appeared and then wipe my blades off on their clothing.

"Well, I expect you know this by now, Akira, but it seems you are critically, lethally unprepared to work with others as a team," said Gilles after catching his breath.

I nodded as I pulled out a fairly large mana stone from within the pile of meat. Even if I had the highest class level of anyone here, that didn't change the fact that I had extremely little teamwork experience.

"Something tells me a half-baked level of teamwork won't cut it against the demons either," Kyousuke added in a measured voice.

He was probably right. I certainly couldn't beat Mahiro on my own, and I might not have even been able to beat Aurum. And trying to work as a team in ways you hadn't practiced in advance, against enemies that were too strong for me to take on myself, was a recipe for disaster.

I needed to remember we were very close to demon territory and that there was at least one demon with magic that would allow them to fly right over here and challenge us. Hell, Latticenail had done it, albeit with the help of a magic flying device. Not that I would say no to the opportunity to reduce their numbers a bit, but that was assuming they wouldn't come in droves. I pondered this for a bit, which I think Gilles interpreted as me feeling miffed as he tried to step in and clear the air.

"I only say that because I know from what you've told us about your previous combat experience that teamwork might be a little... tough for you. But teamwork isn't always strictly advantageous, either. Having more hands on deck to help out is great and everything, but if one person falls out of rhythm, it can mean curtains for the entire party. If there's at least one person who can fend for themselves solo, then hey, at least not everyone will get wiped out, right?"

Gilles smiled, and I felt a chill run down my spine. There was a distinct difference between the core values of someone born in this world and someone born in ours. Don't get me wrong: I didn't want to die, but the thought of going into a battle thinking the other heroes might be expendable sacrifices so long as I alone could survive didn't sit right with me at all.

"Ideally, we'd want everyone to make it out of there alive, obviously," the hero interjected in his usual obnoxious tone. "We can't just let you be *totally* incapable of cooperating with the rest of us."

I grimaced. Yes, I knew that I needed to get better at teamwork, but I found it extremely hard to tell, for example, what Kyousuke was thinking when he took up a given combat position, or why Gilles chose to time his attacks for one opening as opposed to another. "Well, for now, let's just keep doing things the way we have been," I said, shrugging him off. "I still need to get used to how you guys operate, or else I'll never be able to improve."

I turned my back to the three of them. I wondered, had I stayed back at the castle and pled my innocence, if I would have learned to fight as part of a team like them. Not that I thought I made the wrong decision, of course, but I did feel something akin to envy toward them, now that I was being confronted with my own inadequacies.

My Status *as an*
Assassin *Obviously*
Exceeds *the* Hero's

CHAPTER 5

The Final Ingredient

"OKAY, what's next on our list?"

Since we obviously couldn't fight very well having to lug around giant tusks, we'd decided to make a quick pit stop back at home base before heading out again. We had a few accidental monster encounters on the way back, but that couldn't be avoided in this forest. If anything, we were the intruders messing with the native ecosystem here, so I couldn't even blame them.

Gilles spread out the large map of the area we'd been shown a while back on the large dining table while Kyousuke read the next item off the list Noa had given us. "Looks like the next thing we need is something called an 'Orghen's Organ.' But which organ do we *need*? Does it matter, or will any of its innards do?"

I turned to look at Noa, who was leaning against the wall by the door with her arms folded, trying not to get involved. She shook her head. "Nope. I dunno what the word 'organ' refers to in your world, but here, a monster's organ refers to their mana stone. Most monsters can't go on living once it's been removed, you see," she said with a snicker.

Now that she mentioned it, I did recall a few times down in the labyrinth where I ripped out the mana stone of a monster clearly struggling to stay alive, and it died. I'd simply chalked it up to coincidence, but apparently there was a correlation there after all.

"So, all we need to do is find one of these orghen things, and we'll have everything we need to cross over to the demon continent?" asked Kyousuke, dubiously. But...the list did call for only one organ, so presumably that was all we needed.

Amaryllis and Amelia entered the room from a different door, chatting happily. Apparently, they'd gotten on well while we were gone. I knew the fact that Amaryllis had done what she could to medicate and heal the illnesses of the elven captives imprisoned with her made a good impression on Amelia, so I'd had a feeling the two would get along, but I never would have expected them to become good friends.

"It is said that an orghen's mana stone is the largest in the world. If inserted into a magical device, it would generate an unfathomable amount of mana. There's just one problem," Noa said, pausing for effect. "The orghen that live in this forest are constantly on the move, and it is nearly impossible to predict where they might go next. Even I have only encountered one in my lifetime."

With that, Noa walked into the next room (which I believed she'd been using as a storage room) and then dragged a giant object back with her.

"Is that...a *mana stone*?" the hero asked in disbelief.

I honestly couldn't believe it myself. I watched as Noa set the giant mana stone— which was probably as big as I was tall—gently down on the ground.

"This is the only Orghen Organ I own, but it's quite old by now and thus its remaining mana is rather weak. You wouldn't be able to make it all the way across the ocean with this old thing. It's also a bit on the small side," Noa explained, and I nodded in understanding.

So this is the amount of mana you need to cross oceans, eh...? "It sounds like our main issue will be that it's nomadic," I said.

The fact that it never stayed in one place for too long might make finding it an even harder task than slaying it, and we couldn't just split up and scour the entire forest, because there were too many other dangerous monsters lurking about. At the same time, just searching for it blindly without any plan in mind seemed like a fool's errand. I was scratching my head, struggling to come up with any ideas, when I felt a presence approach me. I looked up to see that it was Amaryllis, and she was staring fixedly down at my hand.

"Wh-what's up?" I asked. I'd seen Amaryllis talking with Lia and Amelia plenty, but I hadn't really had a chance to speak with her much since arriving. I wondered what she wanted from me.

"Oh, pardon me. I was just wondering where you got that ring you're wearing," she said, pointing at my finger.

She wasn't pointing to the "ring" Amelia had carved into my finger but at the *actual* ring on my right index finger, which

Crow had given me during our mission to rescue Amelia from her captors. Both rings, as well as the symbol of my pact with Night, were visible, because I always took my gloves and handguards off whenever I was inside. Granted, the symbols of my bonds with Amelia and Night couldn't be removed even if I wanted to, but I just now realized I'd left the ring on since receiving it.

"This? I got it from Crow. What about it?" I asked, and Amaryllis looked down at the ring again—only this time, her gaze was charged with mana.

"What a fascinating magical device you have there. Correct me if I'm wrong, but couldn't you just use that to solve our current predicament?"

I looked down at the ring and remembered what Crow had told me when he gave it to me.

"Wait! Is that a Dowsing Ring?" Noa cried, walking over to examine it closely like Amaryllis. The two of them were getting a little *too* close for comfort, actually.

"Back off, you two," said Amelia grumpily, as if reading my mind. The two smaller girls relented, but their eyes remained locked on my finger. It was a little creepy.

"Right, he said it can guide me to whatever it is I'm searching for," I said. Then, as a test, I closed my eyes and thought long and hard about the large mana stone Noa had shown us. I wanted it.

No, I *needed* it.

"Oho! Incredible! It works just as advertised!" Noa cheered.

I opened my eyes to see a red beam of light shooting out from the ring and onto the wall of the room. Apparently, it was pointing not at the magic stone on the ground but at one that must still have been lodged inside of an orghen, deep in the forest. And just as Noa said, it appeared the beast was constantly on the move, as the beam of light undulated ever so slightly.

It seemed our problems had been solved, and it was all thanks to Crow. I called for the battle unit to head out immediately, but just then, Night and Tsuda came running into the room in a huff. They were supposed to be on a team with Crow and Lia. Was it really a good idea to leave the two of them by themselves?

"Oh, good! They're here! We made it just in time!"

"See, I told you they'd both be here! Maybe you should try listening to me for once!"

"Well, maybe *you* need to learn to sound surer of yourself!!!"

I was surprised to see how well Night seemed to be getting along with the hero's party members after such a short time together. But I really wished he would quit with the hissing because it was *super* obnoxious.

"What's up, you guys?" I asked them. It seemed like they came here looking for someone—maybe on urgent orders from Crow.

They collected their breath and looked at each other, then Night proceeded to explain. *"Hey, hero. Yes, you with the gaping maw. You need to come with us,"* he said. The hero, who'd been standing there with his mouth wide open, dumbfounded, quickly corrected his error.

"...And Noa as well," Tsuda chimed in hesitantly. "We were asked to come get both of you." I tilted my head, puzzled. From

the way they were talking, it didn't sound like Crow had been the one to ask them.

"By whom? My worthless son?" Noa replied.

"Oh, no. By your daughter, actually," Tsuda clarified.

Night had seemingly wanted to leave that part unsaid, but Tsuda let it slip as though it were nothing. *But wait a minute. Isn't Crow's sister supposed to be dead?*

As we all stood there in baffled disbelief, Night graciously sated our curiosity with additional context. *"...We came across a magical device made by the previous hero which has allowed both him and your daughter to materialize in our world, but only for a single day."*

He explained it about as concisely as he possibly could. I had been under the impression it was just as impossible to call back the dead in this world as it was in ours, but apparently the last hero was just *that* talented. I supposed he had to be, considering it wasn't easy for a hero born in this world to stack up against the ones summoned from ours. Noa seemed to buy this explanation as plausible, yet she didn't seem particularly enthused by the chance to speak to her dead daughter. Granted, I hadn't known her long enough to be able to tell what she was thinking from her facial expressions alone, but it was plain to see that she was not delighted, and I had to wonder why.

"I see... Then let us go. Lead the way, you two," she ordered.

"Well, if they called for me too, I guess I'll go. Maybe the previous hero has something really important to tell me," the hero mused.

Noa left the room in order to get ready—presumably to change into some better traveling clothes. The hero was already in his combat outfit, so he and Tsuda headed out first. As soon as they were out the door, the rest of us sat down again.

"Well, now that Satou's out of the picture, I suppose we need to rethink our strategy," said Gilles. Kyousuke and I both nodded.

"For sure. If we tried to stick with our previous battle plan, that'd put way too much of a burden on Kyousuke."

The hero had the best stats of the battle unit aside from me, with pretty solid attack and defense, as well as great observational skills. If I was the lone wolf type who tried to break through the enemy's defenses and finish them off ASAP, he was the type that worked as a team and encouraged his party to try to defeat them together—and Kyousuke and Gilles had both spent their entire journey working with him as part of that team. It wasn't as though we could just force ourselves into a different party makeup, though. Just like how you couldn't put introverts and extroverts together in school and expect things to go well. The only reason their existing party setup had been split into groups this time was because we had a pressing reason to.

Of course, I hadn't seen the other heroes fight as a party very much, but I knew they at least had to be good enough to make it through the forest. From what little I'd heard from Kyousuke, it hadn't been an easy journey, but what I found most interesting was how the noncombatants in the party had stepped up to the plate during the latter half of the trek, when both Kyousuke and the hero were suffering from severe exhaustion. The two of them always overexerted themselves, and Gilles confirmed this to be the case. To be fair, up until now, they'd simply been moving from town to town doing odd jobs for the guild—nothing that could potentially get them killed. But that might be why they didn't know how to reel themselves in during battle, a skill that would have helped them stave off needless exhaustion on their way here. It had even taken me a while to learn that.

"Just thinking in terms of overall combat ability, I think it would be best to move forward with me as the centerpiece of our strategy. Any objections to that idea?"

Both Gilles and Kyousuke shook their heads. From what little Noa told us about the orghen, I had a feeling losing the hero would make it a lot harder to defeat. Thankfully, we had the ring to guide us in its general direction now, but we'd likely encounter a lot more monsters on our way to it, and those battles would wear us down.

"That said," I continued, "I do want to figure out how to best make use of you two and your teamwork. Got any ideas, Gilles?"

"...Hm, perhaps. Let's see what I can come up with."

After we finished our prep meeting and a preliminary gear inspection, we gathered up our equipment and some food and headed out.

"I need an Orghen's Organ... I need one." I said to myself repeatedly, calling forth the beam of red light from the ring. We would follow it exactly where we needed to go. With me taking point, the three of us set off in the direction it indicated. "Wow, it's actually taking us even *closer* to demon territory."

I frowned, realizing this meant the monsters we'd be encountering would be even *stronger*. If an orghen could just come and go as it pleased through this part of the forest, then it had to be an apex predator. Perhaps it was something akin to the Lord of the Forest the hero's party had accidentally awakened. It certainly had to be at least as powerful as the final boss of a labyrinth, like Night had been. I'd gained quite a few levels since facing Night but probably still couldn't come out of a battle like that unscathed. Maybe it was a mistake to not bring Lia and Tsuda with us as well.

"How exactly does Noa expect to make us fly through the air, anyway? I feel like you'd need a small aircraft to carry all of us at once."

With myself, the seven other heroes, and Amelia and Night, there were already ten of us. Add Noa, Crow, and the others to the equation, and we had fifteen. Thanks to the hero, Noa likely had the gist of how aviation worked and could probably buff out the remaining kinks through magic, but it seemed Kyousuke still didn't comprehend why Amelia and I were so confident that Noa would be able to ferry the whole lot of us over to the other shore. As we made our way in the direction of the light, I explained how the Extra Skill World Eyes — which Amelia and I both possessed— worked.

"A skill that allows you to view the stats of another... Fascinating!" said Kyousuke.

"Hang on, are you *serious*?! That's actually *possible*?!" Gilles exclaimed. Maybe Commander Saran hadn't told him about my stats.

Actually, wait a minute. I never even mentioned World Eyes *to Commander Saran, did I? Because at the time, I had no idea what it did.* "Yeah, it's an Extra Skill of mine. I don't know the full extent of its abilities, but as of right now, I can at least say for sure that it lets me view the stats of other people and things. I've never encountered an enemy that was able to prevent me from doing so, at least."

There had been times I'd forgotten to check a foe's stats, or hadn't had enough mana left to do so, but I had yet to meet a foe that could actually block me from using *World Eyes* if I really wanted to. Gilles nodded at last, as though he'd finally wrapped his head around the idea.

"I see. Yes, I suppose with an Extra Skill, it might be possible."

Extra Skills were several orders of magnitude more powerful that regular skills, after all, and it was entirely possible that there existed another Extra Skill out there capable of concealing one's stats from those with World Eyes. Though it seemed Extra Skills were quite rare even among demons, so I wasn't too worried about that at present.

"World Eyes, eh...? I have to wonder if such a skill might be able to see far more than just another person's stats," Kyousuke muttered offhand, scratching his chin.

I couldn't help but flinch, thinking back on the horrific scene I'd witnessed the first time I tried using World Eyes down in the Great Labyrinth of Kantinen—a vision of the other heroes lying dead on the ground while I, alone, stood towering above them. I was so terrified that this vision might one day become a reality that I decided to never use World Eyes for anything but checking an enemy's stats ever again. As a result, I hadn't really leveled the skill up at all. Amelia's was at a much higher level due to her using it frequently.

I could only imagine what all she could see with it now.

"...Who knows? I'm not sure how much more I'd want to see, to be honest with you," I replied simply.

I didn't know why I'd been shown that vision, or whether it was a future that was destined to happen, but despite my curiosity, I knew deep down it would probably be best not to know. I'd learned the hard way I should probably just trust my gut on things like this.

"I tend to agree. I'm not sure why, but it just feels like too much power," said Kyousuke, presumably reacting to what his Intuition skill was telling him. This was a skill of his that had already been at a high level from the moment we were summoned here; my Detect Danger skill was telling me the same thing.

"Glad we agree. Now c'mon, it can't be much farther now."

The red light was still pointing in the same direction, but the fluctuating and bouncing around it was doing had gotten a lot more noticeable. When I said this, my companions both immediately got serious. It randomly occurred to me that both Kyousuke and I had done an awfully good job adapting to this dangerous world.

"The fact that we haven't encountered a single monster thus far worries me. Be on your guard," Gilles said.

We'd all been ready to draw our swords at a moment's notice, yet that hadn't proved necessary. Compared to the amount of attacks we'd suffered on our way to home base, and the fact that we were now far closer to demon territory made me suspect only a few truly powerful monsters roamed these parts. My Detect Presence and Detect Danger skills hadn't alerted me to anything yet, but that was perhaps concerning in and of itself.

"Hey! There it is!"

Now, I was fairly confident in my own skills, though never to the point of relying on them entirely. But the fact of the matter was I was utterly unable to sense this particular monster until it appeared right in front of us.

"Akira!"

Kyousuke cried out in distress to warn me, and I just barely managed to jam my daggers between its claws before it tore me to shreds. However, it had still taken me by surprise, and unable to brace properly for the impact, I was sent flying. I hadn't struggled so hard to block an enemy attack like that since I was still a low-level assassin down in the Great Labyrinth of Kantinen. I hurtled through the air for what felt like ages before finally crashing into a tree some distance away from Kyousuke and Gilles.

"Akira!" Gilles cried out from far away.

"I'm all right! Don't worry about me!" I called back, picking myself up off the ground. Never had I been so grateful for my inhuman defense and stamina before. Despite the incredible velocity with which I'd crashed into the tree, I was able to hop right back up with only a few light scratches.

Given how far away Gilles's voice sounded, it seemed best to operate under the assumption we wouldn't really be able to provide backup for each other during this fight. I could only just see through the trees that there was not just one but two giant monsters over by Gilles and Kyousuke. But just as I was about to dash over there, an even bigger monster stepped directly in my path. And despite being right there in front of me, my Detect Presence and Detect Danger skills weren't responding at all.

We'd been *ambushed*.

They looked nothing like the animalistic monsters we'd encountered before and more resembled the sorts of monsters you might see in fantasy illustrations. They had batlike wings; long, thin arms and legs; and at least ten beady, red, spider-like eyes with which they were glaring down at us. They also had long tentacles dangling down from their mouths, all of which were wriggling and waggling around as though they had minds of their own. They were completely black and utterly repulsive in every single way. Other monsters we'd encountered had been kind of cute in a weird way, but these were just...*not*.

As I watched cautiously, waiting for its next move, I noticed the light from my ring was pointing directly at the one in front of me. "I see. So, you're an orghen, eh?"

I could definitely understand how a monster like this could contain a mana stone as tall as I was. Most of the monsters I'd taken mana stones from had been humanoid, but I could tell from one look that these things were at least as intelligent as people were. They might not be as clever as Night, but they certainly had more wits about them than any of the other enemies we'd faced. Perhaps monsters just looked more disgusting as you got closer to the demon continent. I had dearly hoped the orghen were outliers, though, and that most would be cute and cuddly like Night.

"Whoa!"

As I stood there observing, the orghen had grown impatient and lashed out with its mighty claws. Last time, it had caught me off guard, but this time I was prepared to defend against its attack. Despite having arms only about as thick as my own, a single swipe of its claws was enough to uproot several trees from the immediate vicinity. It was for this reason I opted to try to deflect its attacks rather than block them. Hell, if it hadn't been me who'd taken that last attack, it probably would've ruptured someone's internal organs.

I wondered why it singled me out. We were all equally oblivious to their presence, so surely anyone would have done. And usually, the wild monsters of this forest judged their enemies' abilities on instinct and went for the weakest party members first. For example, all the way to the safe house, monsters were constantly attacking Amaryllis first. So it confused me that these monsters had picked me, whose stats were objectively the highest out of the three of us.

Regardless, after deflecting the attack, I put some distance between me and the monster, and then used World Eyes to take a peek at its stats.

ORGHEN KING

RACE: Monster

HP: 32000/32000   **MP:** 50000/50000

ATTACK: 600000   **DEFENSE:** 45000

SKILLS:

Control (Lv. 7)   Wind Claw (Lv. 5)

Healing Magic (Lv. 6)   Intellect (Lv. 3)

EXTRA SKILLS:

Invisibility   Penetrating Eye

AKIRA ODA

RACE: Human   **CLASS:** Assassin (Lv. 88)

HP: 33650/34600   **MP:** 11700/119000

ATTACK: 25400   **DEFENSE:** 13600

SKILLS:

Mathematics (Lv. 5)   Negotiation (Lv. 5)

Assassin Tools (Lv. 8)   Assassination (Lv. 9)

Curved Swords (Lv. 9)   Short Swords (Lv. 9)

Conceal Presence (Lv. MAX)   Detect Presence (Lv. 9)

Detect Danger (Lv. 9)   Intimidate (Lv. 8)

Roar (Lv. 4)   Dual Blades (Lv. 6)

Mana Control (Lv. 8)   Bewitchment (Lv. 5)

Buff Up (Lv. 2)

EXTRA SKILLS:

Understand Languages   World Eyes (Lv. 2)

Shadow Magic (Lv. 8)

Seeing our stats side by side, I couldn't help but gawk. Its defense was one thing, but how in the hell could it possibly have an *Attack of 600000*? Judging from its name, it was presumably the leader of all the orghens, but even so, its stats were considerably higher than even those of the Demon Lord's daughter. Monsters didn't have classes, so it was difficult to compare them in terms of level, but if they did, this one probably would have been a much higher level than me.

In other words, it was an extremely powerful enemy that even my best attacks might not be enough against. Feeling much more wary all of a sudden, I readjusted my grip on my daggers. I hadn't felt as concerned for my life since I had to duel with the demons, and before that, not since the Great Labyrinth of Kantinen. But despite my anxieties, I still curved my lips up into a defiant smirk. My heart was pounding like crazy, and I could feel the adrenaline coursing through my body. I opened my eyes wide and looked up at the beast, and I could feel my pupils expanding. *Now* this *is what I'm talking about. Finally, a worthy opponent!*

"Mwa ha ha... *HA HA HA!*"

I had completely lost control of my emotions as I brandished the Yato-no-Kami daggers like a beast gone mad.

POV: ASAHINA KYOUSUKE

"*Ha Ha Ha...!*"

After Akira went flying and then entered into a staredown with the monster, Gilles and I looked at each other, both a little unsettled by the sound of faint laughter coming from our stranded companion. Even the monster seemed a little taken aback by Akira's reaction, as it halted for a moment. These monsters seemed awfully humanlike in a lot of ways.

"What's gotten into him?" Gilles asked worriedly, and I shook my head.

Something told me Akira was simply enjoying himself, for whatever reason. I expressed this to Gilles, and he seemed downright confused. Indeed, it was hard to comprehend, but we had no way of knowing why exactly Akira was laughing. All I knew was he was an absolute force to be reckoned with on the battlefield, and so he probably found it fun whenever he got the chance to go up against a real challenge.

"Something tells me we won't each be able to take them down one on one," Gilles said calmly.

I nodded, looking away from Akira (who could probably fend for himself) and turning to face the monsters closer to us. These two were smaller than the one harassing Akira but still quite a bit larger than us. Assuming Akira could handle the big one, we would have to defeat these two on our own. In terms of survivability, it would probably behoove us to bide our time until Akira could back us up, but something told me the monsters wouldn't just wait around for that.

"I'll go first, starting with the left one. Cover me," Gilles said, never taking his eyes off of the monsters.

I held up the Hakuryuu sword I'd brought with me from the castle, its pure white blade shining in the light. Usually, I used a different sword, but for whatever reason, I felt compelled to use this one this time. It was probably my Intuition at work. It was the same skill that had alerted me to the monsters' presence where Akira's Detect Presence and Detect Danger skills had failed, but it also didn't give me any concrete information on where the enemy was located. These enemies were able to conceal themselves from Akira's skills but not Intuition.

"Hyaaaah!!!"

Gilles dodged and weaved through the monster's claw swipes, got up close, and sliced off the tentacles hanging from its mouth. I moved in and used my sword to break its claws to protect Gilles, who then attempted to kick off the ground and, with a mighty leap, decapitate the beast before it had a chance to react. After reaching the peak of his jump, he began hurtling downward with his sword aimed directly at the monster's neck.

"Wait, Gilles!" I cried, sensing something ominous, but Gilles followed through, eager to seize a quick victory.

There was a shrill metallic noise as Gilles's sword snapped in two, right at the center of the blade. It was a strong sword too, tempered by Crow himself, and well cared for. He'd even had Crow take a look at it before we left home base, so there couldn't have been a problem with the sword. Which meant the monster's neck was so tough that the sword simply wasn't strong enough to pierce it. That explained why these monsters were able to come and go as they pleased through this extremely dangerous part of the forest, at least.

His weapon broken, I quickly collected the now-vulnerable Gilles and retreated with him to a distance safe from the two monsters' attacks.

He was silent for a while, perhaps in shock due to having his beloved sword broken so easily, and he simply grasped it in his hands as he allowed me to carry him away. I didn't quite know how to console him, particularly because I had no idea how long he'd been using that sword or just how much it meant to him. The last thing I wanted, however, was for him to snap on me and go for a furious suicide attack with a broken blade.

I always seemed to make things worse in situations like this. Maybe it was because of my soft-spoken nature, or because I struggled to express my thoughts in words, or because my expression was too vacant, but it only ever seemed to make people angrier. In the past, I hadn't even realized what the issue was, only that people seemed to get upset when talking to me, and so I tried to keep my interactions with others to a minimum. Until I met Akira. If he and I hadn't grown close enough for him to feel comfortable pointing these issues out to me, I likely never could have interacted with others normally, and I would certainly not have volunteered to leave the castle with Tsukasa and the others.

I wanted to return the favor to Akira, and more importantly, be of help to him as a true friend, but he was already so strong, and he had Amelia and Night to assist him, so it felt like my help was unnecessary. The least I could do was return the favor to Gilles who'd helped us escape the castle. I removed the sword I wasn't using currently from my belt, sheath and all, and forced it into Gilles's hands. I tried my very best to choose my words carefully so I didn't insult or confuse him.

"Here, take this," I said. "I know you may not have the Curved Swords skill, so it may be a bit cumbersome to use, but it's better than being completely unarmed."

I couldn't allow Gilles to die here, and I couldn't allow myself to die either. I had to save this man however I could. Giving up a sword did mean I wouldn't be able to use my Dual Blades skill, but I would manage. I laid Gilles down in the shadow of a nearby tree, then leapt out in front of the monsters. So long as I swung my sword with the intent to make shallow cuts as opposed to sever, I was fairly confident my blade would not break in the same way. And thankfully, katanas were uniquely skilled at slicing things up as opposed to chopping them off. It had come in handy when we had to fight a large turtle-like beast in this same forest with a hard shell. No matter the monster, and no matter how thick its skin, there would always be a soft spot to exploit.

The monsters, apparently not having expected me to return, quickly lunged out with their tentacles and claws. They'd moved a bit from where we'd previously clashed, presumably on their way to help the bigger one fight Akira. As soon as they recognized I was alone this time, they approached me cautiously, probably convinced I was trying to serve as a decoy. While they were clearly more intelligent than most monsters, they were by no means as smart as humans or Night. If I were them, and I realized there was a third threat who was now unaccounted for, I would have congregated around the big one to help take out the largest threat, Akira.

The fact that they were not doing this told me they had decided the two of them could easily take me down or that they were confident Gilles was no longer a threat. Another possibility (that I didn't really want to consider) was that they had a skill like Akira's that allowed them to view others' stats and had decided they could beat me based on that. There was nothing worse than allowing an enemy to see your hand prematurely.

"...Let's do this," I whispered to myself, after taking a deep breath.

It was my normal pre-match ritual that I did between bouts during kendo meets. During team matches, I got encouragement from my teammates, but in singles matches, this was how I pumped myself up. I was a little surprised I hadn't done it even once since coming to this world, despite having taken part in actual combat almost every day. It was a simple gesture, and yet I could feel it calming my heart and mind. Obviously, a school kendo match and an actual life-or-death battle were two very different things, but for me, they may as well have been exactly the same.

"Hup!"

I started with the orghen's legs and quickly discovered the shins and knees were much too hard for my blade to do much damage. However, I was able to slice right through the back of its knees, and the monster cried out in pain and fell, tumbling to its knees—implying that I had cut right through muscle. It could no longer support its massive weight. The monster's face was now within reach, and I used my sword to trace around it, looking for any soft spots.

"Aha! Now I've got you."

It all happened in about a second. The other monster, apparently not able to keep up, seemed utterly astonished when its friend fell to its knees, and stood there, blinking. I examined the areas I'd just sliced and confirmed my theory that, while the creature's vitals were well guarded, their joints and eyes were relatively soft and vulnerable. If my sword was to break, I could always switch to using two daggers like Akira.

Feeling reinvigorated, I gripped my katana with both hands. This time, I would cut true.

"It seems I might just be able to take down both of these things by myself after all!"

POV: ODA AKIRA

AFTER A HEARTY CACKLE, I licked my lips. As much as I wanted to just let loose the full power of my Shadow Magic, I couldn't deny the possibility I might lose control of it, and then we'd have another situation like when a past hero accidentally destroyed half the demon continent on our hands. I needed to keep my cool, especially since Gilles and Kyousuke were here with me.

"Shadow Magic, activate."

I hoped they'd understand me going overboard— at least a little bit. My shadows wriggled and squirmed violently in accordance with the heightened tension I was feeling. To consume such gigantic monsters with considerably smaller shadows would take an exorbitant amount of mana, however, because the creature wasn't going down without a fight.

"Shadowstep."

Gripping both daggers, I lunged at the beast. I knew it would be difficult to drag it in while it still drew breath, so I was hoping to find another solution. Really, all I needed was the giant mana stone, so I was happy to let my shadows devour the rest.

I swung my daggers at the monster's neck but was quickly thwarted by its massive claws. However, just after this, the monster stopped dead in its tracks. The shadow that should have been behind it was no longer there, having been absorbed by my Shadow Magic, which proceeded to impale the monster from behind. When the shadows came bursting out the front, they grazed my cheek. Shadowstep was a technique that connected my shadow with the shadow of my opponent and brought theirs under my control. Because it required getting up close and personal, however, and the position of the sun wasn't always ideal, I had scarce few opportunities to use it.

"Oh, come on, guys. Quit messing around," I told the shadows as they tickled my cheek.

This was a life-or-death situation, and their childish behavior had just destroyed my focus. The shadows quickly drooped as if depressed and slithered out from the orghen's stomach. The monster began coughing up dark red blood; I was a little surprised at how close the color looked to human blood.

I watched as the gaping hole in its stomach writhed a bit before sealing back up.

"Oh, right... I forgot you can use healing magic," I said, rebuking myself for the lapse. It seemed much closer to regeneration skill than simple healing magic—but I suppose I should have expected no less from a "King."

Because I couldn't just obliterate the thing and risk damaging the mana stone inside, the only way I could prevent it from regenerating over and over was to slice its head off in one fell swoop. There was a good chance it could regenerate entire limbs, after all. I tried my best to come up with a plan, all the while deflecting its claws and cutting through tentacles that tried to wrap themselves around me. The one major downside to having broken the Yato-no-Kami in two was that my blades had a significantly shorter reach. My attacks simply couldn't hit my foes unless I got right up in their faces. Thankfully, I had my Shadow Magic to cover me for just such cases.

I didn't think there even existed another type of magic as easy to use as Shadow Magic, provided you had sufficient mana reserves. Most monsters were easy enough for it to devour, and it converted them right back into mana, which allowed me to get back at least part of the casting cost. They could slice, skewer, and eat up anything in their path, and they could even be used as a shield if need be. They were extremely faithful but also a little playful at times. Sure, most people probably couldn't get past the mana consumption problem, but I had to wonder what might happen if someone with nearly infinite mana reserves like Amelia got ahold of this skill. Though with nothing to stop her, that might be a bad idea, as the shadows might just swallow up the entire world (not that I think she'd let that happen, of course).

I fended off the tentacles with my dagger and waited for an opening. It would be rather simple to just slice them all off as they came, then go for its throat, but I was beginning to feel uneasy about the orghen's actions. I didn't know why, but when an opportunity to slit its throat finally presented itself, I resisted the urge and leapt out of the way.

"...I get it now. You're trying to get me to destroy my weapon, aren't you?" I muttered as I landed on a high tree branch. The orghen's many eyes widened as though it understood my words.

Every monster I'd encountered in the Great Labyrinth of Kantinen with the "King" suffix attached to its name had been a real tough contender. Perhaps due to their greater intellect, they always had a bunch of goons with them that they could order around and arrange into battle formations, and they would often wait in the little nooks and crannies for a chance to jump out and ambush me while I was taking a break. You had to always be on your guard.

And yet, this Orghen King had higher stats and skill levels than anything I'd ever encountered, so I couldn't simply try to go for its neck to finish off the threat. Come to think of it, the fact that it had those easily cuttable tentacles covering its throat was a bit strange—almost like it was trying to lure people into thinking its neck was vulnerable.

The most obvious answer was that it was a ploy to destroy its foe's weaponry. There were warriors who fought using their bare hands, but they wouldn't dare to go up against the orghen's sharp claws unarmed. Most foes would inevitably try to go for the finishing blow and take off its head and get their swords broken in the process. Many lost their nerve when they lost their weapons, and that would give the monster the perfect opportunity to take them out. Even I was a little flustered by how confident I was that I could take the thing down, only to be proven wrong. So that was what made this one a "King." I didn't know how it could accurately predict the way humans would try to combat it, but the strategy presumably worked on monsters as well.

"Sorry, big guy, but I'm afraid you underestimated me. Shadow-Clad!"

Having kept my shadows pooled inside my own natural shadow for a while in order to conserve mana, I now had them wrap themselves around my daggers. This was a technique I hadn't used since my duel with Kilika, yet it seemed like the most effective solution available to me right now. After all, I knew its neck was sturdy, and that trying to cut it would only break my daggers. But with Shadow Magic enveloping the blades, they became several orders of magnitude more deadly and would surely be able to cut right through the Orghen King's neck.

I kicked off from the branch I'd been standing on. Seeing that I was making a break for its neck, the monster shot out its tentacles and claws, all of which were easily swallowed up by my shadows and disappeared on contact. The path to its neck was now unobstructed, so I drove my daggers down into it. There was a satisfying *crunch*, and a moment later, the Orghen King's head was divorced from its shoulders. I landed on the ground behind the beast and called off my Shadow Magic as I turned to hear the beast let out its final death wails. As soon as I confirmed it had stopped moving altogether, I let out a heavy sigh of relief.

That had taken a lot more mana than I anticipated—things could have gotten a little dicey if it had resisted any longer. I was utterly exhausted from the battle and mana consumption, but I still had to dig out the mana stone from its body and somehow carry it back to the safe house. Speaking of which, how were Kyousuke and Gilles faring? The fact that the two smaller orghens hadn't come to the King's aid suggested they'd already dispatched them, but I figured it would be a good idea to reconnect with them ASAP, just in case.

I quickly carved out the mana stone from the Orghen King (which, again, was larger than my entire body) and headed to where they had been to find that they had only just finished their battle. Kyousuke was so covered in blood that I wondered how he'd taken the beasts down, and Gilles looked a bit sullen, but I was relieved to see them both safe. Neither of them had a skill like World Eyes, so they couldn't have known for sure that the beasts were in fact Orghens, so they'd just destroyed them, mana stone and all. I was surprised to hear that Kyousuke had taken it down by searching around for the monster's soft spots and then driving his sword all the way through. That must have been why he was drenched in so much blood.

Gilles's sword had broken against one of their necks, I learned, so Kyousuke had given him one of his own swords. Then, he took down both orghens without even using his Dual Blades skill. Gilles had still not recovered from the shock of his trusty weapon breaking and was just kind of spacing out. Thinking back on how it felt at first to see the Yato-no-Kami split in two to form my daggers, I could certainly understand the feeling.

Kyousuke gathered up the fragments of their mana stones (which were still far bigger than anything you'd find down in a labyrinth) and put them in a bag. Then as we were about to head home, I watched his face twitch when he saw the massive mana stone I was going to lug back. It had been difficult enough just to carry it over to where they were standing, so I had to wrap my black scarf around it in order to form a makeshift sling. Thank God I always wore that thing.

"That thing's *huge.*"

"I know..." I sighed with a nod.

I could already tell that it was going to be backbreaking work getting it to home base. Even with two other people to help carry it. Gilles seemed to falter a bit when I asked for his help, and while it was certainly possible for just Kyousuke and I to carry it, we wouldn't be able to react quickly in the event of a monster ambush, and there was a chance the mana stone could get broken in a skirmish.

As the two of us struggled to think of a solution, there was a rustling sound from a nearby thicket. I assumed it was a monster, perhaps smelling the blood on Kyousuke's body. He and I quickly got into combat positions but let down our guard upon seeing what actually came out to greet us.

"Oh, it's just another Rabbot."

The Rabbots were a series of sentry robots Noa had created to guard our home base. With both long-range and short-range combat abilities, as well as self-regeneration functionality and poison with every one of its attacks, they were devilish little things that only exemplified Noa's crafty personality. I thought it unfortunate she couldn't come up with a name for them that was a little less lame, but they were excellent security guards. We hadn't encountered any monsters since we got to the safe house thanks to them, which had made it a lot easier to relax and feel safe there, and I'd noticed the other heroes were very grateful for that as well.

As I stared at the Rabbot, I noticed something seemed a little off about it. The robot before us had a different chassis from the Mk 11 we'd encountered the first time we met Noa. The Mk 11 was a bit slimmer, with protections for its joints and a regeneration function that made its body very tough to scratch. But this one was covered in scratches and had clearly been made with much stronger arms. Though it also looked like it had been well taken care of, as there were traces of scratches that had been obviously tended to.

"It says 'Rabbot Mk 3' right here," said Kyousuke, who'd gone around to check its back.

I went back there with him and verified that the model's name was indeed handwritten there in big, boorish letters and scrawled in childlike handwriting. I was beginning to second guess my assertion that it had been well taken care of.

"I think this might have been the robot that ferried us back to the safe house after we collapsed from exhaustion," Kyousuke said.

Which meant this was likely a specialized robot that Noa made for hauling heavy objects around. As if to prove this theory, the Rabbot walked over and picked the giant mana stone we'd been struggling to carry right off the ground, and, using another set of arms that came out of its back, it picked up the bag of mana stone fragments as well. With its help, we'd be able to make our way back to home base without having to worry about being taken unawares.

With me in the lead, Kyousuke bringing up the rear, and the Rabbot and a still-depressed Gilles in the middle, we began making our way back to home base. Gilles didn't say a word the whole way and simply held his sword close to his chest. When we arrived at our destination, we found that Noa and everyone else had already made it back.

"Hey, good, you're back... Wait, what the? Gilles?" the hero asked.

"He broke his sword. Take him over to Crow, would you? So, how'd your meeting with the previous hero go?" I asked.

"Later! Gilles comes first."

I couldn't know how much that sword meant to Gilles, but there was nothing I could do to help him with that. He needed to speak with a proper blacksmith.

Upon entering the building, Amelia—who had been busy making dinner with the rest of the girls—quickly ran over to greet me, happy to see that I was safe. Night hopped up onto my shoulders and smiled contently. I gave him some chin scritches, and he purred like a proper house cat. I couldn't express how grateful I was to have found two wonderful companions, especially after being lost and alone when I ran away from Retice Castle.

Noa said she wanted to finish up with us before dinner, so everyone except for Gilles and Crow headed back outside. With something like a blueprint in hand, she led the way to the same open area she'd used to "train" the other heroes. All the materials had been gathered there.

Everyone's jaws dropped when they saw the massive mana stone, which was a fair bit bigger than the one Noa had shown us as an example. The moment Noa realized she'd be able to use that stone (possibly the largest in the world) however she saw fit, her eyes started glimmering greedily, and for once she was acting the age she actually looked. I asked about the mana stone she already had, and she told me that she'd gotten it from fighting a regular orghen with her bare hands. I didn't know whether to be impressed by her confidence or terrified by her insanity. Still, that at least explained why she hadn't warned us about their unique strategy of trying to break their foes' weapons—she couldn't have known that if she'd only challenged one unarmed. I mentioned this to her, and she suddenly recalled just how thick the monster's neck had been, and nodded in understanding as she began to go over all of the materials once more. When she reached the last item on the list, the "Orghen Organ," she nodded and turned to face us.

"We have everything we need now to ferry you all across continents. Now it's time to start building," she said.

Apparently, we were all going to get to witness her Extra Skill. She asked everyone to take a few steps back, but the other heroes seemed too confused trying to figure out what she was about to do, so I had to help pull them back. After confirming we were all a safe distance away, Noa held out her hands toward the pile of materials and called forth her Extra Skill.

"Activating Extra Skill... *Creation!* Let the construction commence."

The materials glowed and floated up into the air, where they were brought together and began to glow even brighter, to the point that I had to close my eyes and turn away for fear of going blind.

"...It is done," she announced, letting out a sigh of relief.

I opened my eyes, unsure how much time had passed. There in the middle of the clearing, , where a pile of raw materials had been only moments ago, was a large, fully-fledged ship. But not just any ship—one with *wings*. It wasn't quite as big as the *Searunner* which had taken us from the elven domain to the land of Brute, but it was still more than large enough to hold our entire party. I was at a loss for words. On further inspection, I realized the outer hull was made from the shells of those highly defensive turtle monsters she had me hunt dozens of earlier.

"This is ridiculous, dude..."

Never in my wildest dreams did I imagine her making something *this* impressive. Noa nodded, pleased by my genuine admiration of her abilities.

"It's my first time making something so large, you know," she said, explaining that she'd run test after test based on the hero's explanation of aviation before finally arriving at the final

blueprints. It was no wonder she'd locked herself up in her room the entire time we were off gathering materials. "My original plan was to try to make something that could get you to the very edge of the Volcano continent, but because you brought back a mana stone far bigger than predicted, you might very well have enough fuel to make it all the way to the very center of the continent. But, of course, I know no journey is without its unexpected setbacks."

Ignoring how ominous that last bit sounded, I realized the reason she'd designed it like a traditional ship was so that it could remain afloat in the event it fell from the sky into the ocean, in which case the aquatic functionality would automatically kick in—though I prayed it would never come to that.

"Man, I'm surprised you had enough mana to create something so massive," I said in awe, walking up next to her as she gazed upon her creation with glee. I'd been under the impression that all Extra Skills used an exorbitant amount of mana.

"Are you kidding? Of *course* I didn't have enough for that," she said, shrugging her shoulders as though I'd just said the dumbest thing imaginable.

But then, how did she do it? I asked this aloud, and she pointed over at the Rabbot Mk 3 that was standing a little ways away, carrying something fairly massive in its arms.

"I used the remaining mana from the Orghen Organ I already had in my possession. It was close, but it was just barely enough to get the job done."

It was right after the other heroes walked inside the ship to check out its interiors that I noticed she was teetering unsteadily on her feet, and I quickly reached out my left arm to support her. She was probably suffering from serious mana exhaustion but wanted to put up a tough front so the other heroes didn't start thinking she was any less of a badass.

"Sorry," she said.

"Don't worry about it," I replied. "But...what were you planning to do in the event that it *wasn't* enough mana? Just die?"

I'd suffered from severe mana exhaustion before, so I knew how scary it could be. She was trying her best to act like she was fine, but she was definitely in danger back there.

"No, I have no intention of dying until I see my son through his final moments. That said, I'm quite grateful to you for helping avenge my daughter, you know," she said, refusing to stop talking even though she was surely on the brink of passing out.

Amelia and Night both tried to chime in, but I raised a hand to stop them, feeling it would be best to at least hear her out.

"It should have been me, you know," she went on. "I should have been the one to kill that worthless man, instead of making my son waste so many years of his precious remaining time in this world. It seems all I ever do is make mistakes," she said, starting to nod off, and I let out a sigh.

Talk about your dysfunctional families. "Y'know, Crow told me you only drank that immortality potion by accident, but you did it on purpose, didn't you?"

I didn't know if Noa just couldn't bear the thought that, as a human, she would die before she got to see her still-unborn beastfolk son grow up, or if there were complications during childbirth on account of her son being of a different race. This world's medicine probably also wasn't nearly as advanced back then as it was now.

"You're right. I did. I don't know what came over me, even knowing that there was a good chance we both might die if I didn't drink the potion. I feel terrible about it to this day. But seeing him alive and well has always been my greatest source of happiness," she said before finally losing her grip on consciousness.

My left arm alone couldn't support her entire weight, so she started falling—but a pair of arms was there to catch her.

"...Why don't you try saying that to my face sometime, you old hag?"

Crow had caught his mother and was now carrying her limp body in both arms. I couldn't quite make out his face through the shadow of his bangs, but it seemed Noa's words had quite an effect on him. Honestly, I was just trying to goad an answer out of her as a bit of a trick before I noticed Crow walking out the back door, but hey—if it solved some family issues for them, I'd consider it a win.

"Wow, Akira. You're more of a troublemaker than I thought," said Amelia.

I pretended not to know what she was talking about and simply followed Crow as he carried Noa toward the ship.

"What, you didn't know? Master's always been like that."

"Oh, I knew, all right. Remember, I've known him longer than *you* have, Night."

As the two of them bickered over who knew me best, we stepped inside the airship Noa had created. I would have really preferred to not let them ruin this touching mother-son moment.

"The thing that terrifies me more than anything else in the world...is when I try to reach out for something and my fingers touch nothing."

I thought back on that night, when, in the dim moonlight, I saw Crow at his most vulnerable, when he said those words to me.

"Well, I'm glad they found something to hold onto this time."

A few hours later, as the full moon shone down over the land, we set forth on the final leg of our journey. Our destination: the land of demons.

AFTERWORD

THANK YOU SO, SO MUCH for picking up this fourth volume in the *Assassin* series. I know it's been quite a while between the publication of the third volume and now, and I have to admit that even I didn't think a fourth one was going to happen for a while, so I'm very pleased to be writing this right now to say the least. And of course, I'm already hard at work penning a fifth volume as we speak!

Incidentally, I've been spending a lot of time these days looking at travel brochures and websites, longing for a chance to get away from it all in our current day and age. Places like the star-shaped fort in Hakodate, Nagoya and Ise, Katsurahama and Izumo... I know it seems hard to imagine there ever being an end to COVID-19 right now, but I've been planning out all sorts of trips to places I'd like to visit as soon as we can get back to a place where traveling freely around the country feels safe and secure. Honestly, just looking through the brochures and planning out hypothetical itineraries is a fun pastime in itself—I'd highly recommend it, if you're ever feeling bored!

Once again, I'd like to thank Tozai for all the wonderful illustrations that adorn the pages of this volume, my managing editor, my proofreader, and last but not least, Hiroyuki Aigamo, who's done such a great job adapting my story into manga format. I hope you'll all look forward to what the future holds for the *Assassin* franchise.